W9-BWW-872

8487

REVENGE IS SWEET

Valessa held on to the railings and bent forward to throw herself head first into the waves...she wished she had never consented to take part in such a degrading Charade for the entertainment of Lady Barton's house guests but, penniless and starving, she had little option.

Now she was aboard a yacht, legally married to the autocratic Marquis of Wyndonberry who hated her as the cause of his humiliation. If only she could explain how she had been used as an instrument of revenge by the woman he scorned. Prepared to be blackmailed by a scheming fortune hunter, the Marquis was confronted by someone young and very innocent. A girl who was prepared to die to set him free...

WITHDRAWN

REVENGE IS SWEET

Revenge is Sweet

by
Barbara Cartland

MAGNA PRINT BOOKS
Long Preston, North Yorkshire,
England.

British Library Cataloguing in Publication Data.

Cartland, Barbara, *1902—*
   Revenge is sweet.
   I. Title
   823.912 (F)

   ISBN 1-85057-882-6
   ISBN 1-85057-883-4 pbk

First Published in Great Britain by Pan Books Ltd., 1988

Copyright © 1988 by Cartland Promotions

Published in Large Print 1990 by arrangement with the copyright holder and Fiord Forlag A/S.

All rights reserved. No part of this publication may be reproduced, stored in a retrieval system, or transmitted in any form or by any means, electronic, mechanical, photocopying, recording or otherwise, without the prior permission of the Copyright owner.

Printed and bound in Great Britain by
Redwood Press Limited, Melksham, Wiltshire.

AUTHOR'S NOTE.

Steeplechasing was originally an impromptu horse race with some visible church steeples as a goal.

It was a horse race across open country, now it is run on a course with artificial fences.

Steeplechase and hurdle racing trace their origin to the chase and the Field of War where the necessity to clear formidable obstacles was the object of the exercise.

The earliest horse race recorded in England was one held about A.D 210 at Wetherby, North Yorkshire, among Arabians brought to Britain by Lucius Septimius Severus (A.D 146-211 Emperor of Rome.)

In the Georgian days, the Bucks and Beaux used to have midnight steeplechases which were terribly dangerous because they had often drunk far too much and gave themselves ridiculous handicaps like riding blindfold or with one arm tied to their sides.

The Grand National Steeplechase which had begun in 1837 as the Grand Liverpool Steeplechase became the most famous and important

NEWARK PUBLIC LIBRARY - NEWARK, OHIO 43055

3 2487 00113 8487

steeplechase through the world.

The course, an irregular triangle, must be covered twice for a distance of four miles, 856 yards, and a total of 30 jumps among which the most spectacularly hazardous are those known as Becher's Brook and Valentine's Brook.

The Jockey Club which controls all the Horse-racing in England was formed in 1750 to 51.

CHAPTER ONE
1836

Valessa stood looking out of the window.

It was a warm day for the end of November and the sun was shining.

There had been a touch of frost during the night, but not enough to stop the hunting. The trees were turning to red and brown and the leaves beneath them were a carpet of the same colours.

'It is a nice day for dying,' Valessa said aloud.

She had a sudden impulse after all to stay alive, then knew it was impossible.

She could not go on as she was and she knew the sudden craving for life was merely because she had eaten something.

When she had decided yesterday there was nothing else for her to do but die, she had thought she would at least have a good breakfast.

Otherwise it was unlikely she would be able to walk as far as the river or if she got there, to have the strength of will to throw herself into it.

She had therefore bartered her last sheet with the exception of those she was using, for two eggs.

For a pillow-case that had been embroidered by her mother she received three slices of bread and a tiny piece of butter.

She would dress first, she decided, then go down to the kitchen to eat what to her would be a feast.

But when she awoke she was so hungry that she had gone downstairs in her nightgown.

She had eaten the eggs and the hot toast, thinking it was the most delicious meal she had ever had.

There had been nothing for her to drink but water which at least she had been able to heat in the kettle on the fire.

She had, she thought been very intelligent about the fires.

The only thing left that was free was the dead wood from the trees which grew all around the house.

She had managed to have a fire in her bedroom as well as the one in the kitchen.

She kept the bedroom fire going all night.

In the morning she relit the fire in the kitchen by carrying a piece of burning wood in a scuttle downstairs.

The warmth from the fires had been, she

thought, the only thing that had kept her alive.

She had had less and less to eat until she realised there was nothing more to sell.

Unless she wished to die slowly of starvation, it would be best for her life to end in the river.

It hardly seemed possible that everything should have happened so quickly, and the house which had been her home was now an empty shell.

There was nothing in the rooms but the marks left by the pictures on the walls.

The pieces of carpet on the floor were too threadbare for anybody to wish to take them away.

It had once been a place of laughter and happiness.

They were poor, but there had always been, although it was plain, plenty to eat.

Looking back, she thought that no man could have been more handsome and attractive than her father.

Yet she supposed he was to blame for everything that had happened.

It had all started long before she was born when Charles Chester had quarrelled with his father.

'I am damned if I will go into the Army!' he had declared. 'You have treated me as if I was a raw recruit ever since I was a child! I am

11

going to enjoy life and see the world!'

'If you do not do as I tell you, I will cut you off without a penny!' his father had roared.

Charles however was determined to do what he wanted.

He had run away from home two days later, taking with him all the cash he could find.

He had also taken, and this was more serious, a neighbour's daughter, Elizabeth, whom he had been courting secretly for over a year.

He had nothing to offer her, and to speak of his love to her father would, he knew, just be a waste of words.

He therefore told Elizabeth he was leaving.

But when he kissed her she knew that nothing mattered but him.

They went off quietly, not even thinking of the chaos they left behind them.

On Elizabeth's part it was certainly very serious.

Her father had given his approval to her engagement to a man of social importance who was far older than she was.

The marriage was to have taken place in two weeks' time.

When Elizabeth left, on Charles's instructions she took with her the jewellery which had been left to her by her mother.

Also the jewels which had been given to her

as a wedding-present.

'We might as well be "hung for a sheep as a lamb",' Charles had grinned, 'and if they attempt to catch up with us, which is very doubtful, we shall be on the high seas.'

'Where are we going?' Elizabeth asked a little belatedly.

'As far as I am concerned, to Paradise,' he answered, 'but actually, I thought first we would visit Egypt and see the Pyramids.'

Elizabeth knew all she wanted was to be with him.

When they had left they did not care about the fury of their parents nor did they think of the shocked exclamations of their other relatives.

They were, as it happened, comparatively well off.

Elizabeth's mother had left her money besides her jewellery in her will.

It amounted to nearly £300 a year and it enabled them to travel to a number of distant and unusual places.

Only just before Valessa was born did they come back to England.

They made no attempt to get in touch with their relatives who would not have spoken to them anyway.

Charles found a small black and white

timbered house in Leicestershire which he was able to buy for what he called 'a song'.

Elizabeth made it very comfortable, and after Valessa was born they stayed there for nearly two years.

Then Charles began to get restless and they set off again on their travels, taking their daughter with them.

Before she was old enough to understand what was happening, Valessa was happy to ride a camel or to climb a mountain because her father was determined to reach the top of it.

She had also travelled down crocodile-infested rivers and explored parts of Africa.

She had grown used to eating strange foods, sleeping in a tent, sometimes even in a cave.

Then they would be back in England where there were horses that she learned to ride as well as her father did.

It was horses with which he was obliged to fill his life when Elizabeth became not well enough to travel outside England.

She had caught several tropical fevers unknown to doctors and very weakening.

It was now impossible for her to do any more than keep the house comfortable for her husband and daughter.

It was fortunate from Charles's point of

view that as she grew older Valessa was able to help him.

She could eventually train the horses he broke in almost as well as he could.

The horses were to be his only source of income when Elizabeth died suddenly and quietly in her sleep.

Valessa could hardly believe it.

One moment her mother was with them, laughing, her eyes filled with love for her handsome husband.

The next she was being carried in a small coffin into the Churchyard.

It was after Elizabeth's death that everything went wrong.

Later Valessa knew it was a tragedy, owing to the way in which her grandmother had made her will.

It allowed her father control of the capital on which they lived.

It took him three years to spend every penny of it.

First, it was expended on the horses he bought, patronising Tattersall's instead of the Horse Fairs as he had done in the past.

Then, and Valessa knew it was because he was lonely, he took to gambling.

There were two big houses in the neighbourhood where he had friends.

He would not introduce them to her, and they would certainly not have been accepted by her mother.

They were hard-drinking, hard-riding men who enjoyed playing cards for high stakes.

They would, after they had a lot to drink, bet on two flies crawling up a window.

It was too late to do anything about it when Valessa, having just reached the age of eighteen, found that her father had no money.

What he did have was a multitude of debts.

It was then because the Duns were at the door that he began to sell everything in the house.

It was agonising for Valessa to see first the pretty gilt-framed mirrors that her mother had loved taken down from the walls.

Then she found that the French *secretaire* at which her mother had written her letters had vanished overnight.

The rugs they had brought back from Persia were rolled up and taken away in a cart.

'We cannot go on like this, Papa!' Valessa had said finally.

'I know, my poppet,' he had replied, 'and I am deeply ashamed of myself!'

Then he had laughed his carefree laughter which everybody who met him found infectious.

'I am going to a party tonight,' he said, 'and I have a feeling I shall win the jackpot.'

'Oh...no...Papa!' Valessa exclaimed.

But she knew it was no use arguing with him. He hated the emptiness and quietness of the house now that her mother was no longer there.

She knew that he would be the life and soul of any party he went to which was why he had so many invitations.

She only wished they were from people whom her mother would have liked.

Alternatively, that they would perhaps occasionally include her.

She was grown up, but she saw no one except the people in the village and Little Fladbury was a very small one.

There was of course the Parson, who had given her lessons and as he was a very erudite man she was well educated in the Classics, and of course, the Scriptures.

There was the School-Mistress who had taught her mathematics and geography when she was not busy with the village children who had no wish to learn anything.

But more important than anything else there was her mother's library, which was surprisingly large for such a small house.

Her mother had collected the books from all over the world because she loved reading.

17

She had taught Valessa French, Italian and also Spanish when they were travelling.

When they returned home she would insist on her learning to read the books of the country she had visited.

Valessa had a good brain and was very quick at picking things up and she could chatter away to her mother in different languages.

She would also read aloud the books that filled the shelves.

The books were kept in what was called 'The Study', which was a small room, and the only one left where the walls were still furnished.

When her father was killed, Valessa was sure it was intentional. He had been riding home from the party at which he had expected to win the jackpot.

Instead, she learned later, he had lost a large sum of money he did not possess.

She never knew if it was because he was ashamed to tell her about it, or whether he could not face being ostracised by his so-called 'friends'.

A gambling debt was a debt of honour.

Either way she was sure his death was deliberate.

Granted, he had had a lot to drink, but he had put his horse at an insurmountable jump.

He had fallen, as was inevitable, and broken his neck.

It was then that Valessa's world came to an end.

Her father's tailor took the Dining-Room table, the chairs, the sideboard, and grumbled that it was not enough.

His Wine Merchant collected anything of value out of the Drawing-Room.

His Saddler took the pictures on the stairs and the one of her mother which had hung in the Study.

The bedroom furniture was collected by another creditor.

All that was left was Valessa's own bedroom, and a few thing they had treated with scorn.

It was these however that had saved her for the last six months from starving.

First she sold off piece by piece anything the villagers wanted.

They paid a few shillings for the little Dresden china figures and the statues of heathen gods which her father had collected on his travels.

When they were all gone she was reduced to bartering the blankets and sheets for food.

She had known then that everything—the entire contents of the house, would come to an end sooner or later.

It was only at the beginning of this week however that she had faced the fact that she must die.

There was no possible way she could earn money, and certainly nobody in the village wanted her when they were poor themselves.

The 'Big House' as it was called, where the Squire had once lived, was empty, and had been for years.

The villagers subsisted on what they could grow and sell in the market and the town in which it took place on Saturdays was three miles away.

Valessa thought that if she had some money to pay the fare, she might travel to London and see if she could find employment in some capacity or other.

Then she doubted if anyone would engage her and she was too frightened to venture out alone.

It had been different when she was travelling with her father and mother.

Then she had been protected and looked after.

In the last year before her mother became ill she had been aware that men looked at her in what to her was a frightening manner.

They not only bought her chocolates and other small presents, but they would put their arms around her and try to kiss her if her father had not interfered.

'You leave my daughter alone!' he would say.

'She is too pretty,' one man had replied. 'You will have to keep her in a cage, Charlie, when she gets a bit older!'

'I will certainly keep her locked away from Casanovas like you!' her father answered.

Valessa remembered everybody laughing.

After that she had been sent to bed early when her father and mother entertained.

When they were in France she was never allowed to go out alone without somebody being with her.

As she looked in the mirror she thought it was doubtful if anybody now would think her pretty.

She had grown so thin that her eyes were far too big for her face.

Because she was permanently hungry, it was difficult to smile and quite impossible to laugh.

Her hair had in the past always seemed to shimmer as if the sunshine was in it.

While still very long, it was now dull and limp.

There was no longer the sparkle in her eyes which were like her mother's.

Slowly, because it was too much effort to move quickly, even though she was feeling well-fed, Valessa began to dress.

Her clothes, which were all old and thread-bare, were hanging in the wardrobe.

She wondered which would looked best when, sooner or later, they would pull her out of the river.

She felt it was likely that some children would be the first to see her, or perhaps it would be one of the farmers looking for a hare or a rabbit to fill the pot.

Valessa had tried to set up a snare for the rabbits in the garden but she had not been successful.

All she had caught was a magpie which she was sure was a sign of bad luck, and when she turned it loose it flew away.

Afterwards she thought she could have eaten it, but doubted if it would have been very tasty.

She took down from the wardrobe what was 'the best of a bad bunch'.

It was a gown which had been her mother's and it was too big for her, but she thought at least she would look decent when she was dead.

She had sold everything but her mother's clothes had fetched very little.

She knew that the only reason why she had any of her own gowns left was that nobody was thin enough to wear them.

The only decent thing left in her wardrobe

was a warm coat, that she intended to wear as she walked to the river.

She had thought of exchanging it for a piece of meat to go with the eggs she had just eaten.

Then she was afraid that if it was a cold day she might collapse before she reached her destination.

Anyway, the weight of the coat when wet would make her drown more quickly than she would without it.

She had never learned to swim and the river, swollen from the rain that had fallen the previous month, was very deep just before it reached the weir.

Someone had once said that drowning was 'a quick and pleasant way of dying'.

Valessa had heard also that your life passed before your eyes like a kaleidoscope displaying your sins and your virtues.

She did not think when she thought about it that she had many sins but perhaps as they appeared in front of her, she might be surprised.

She buttoned her gown and tidied her hair in the mirror, then walked resolutely back to the wardrobe to take down her coat.

By now she knew it must be getting on for noon, and as there was nothing to eat for a midday meal, the sooner she was in the river the better.

She had just lifted down the coat when she heard, to her surprise, a knock on the front door.

She wondered who it could possibly be.

In the last week no one had called at the house and the only time she spoke to anyone was when she had gone into the village.

It was about a quarter-of-a-mile away, and she had found it too far.

Yesterday she had made a special effort to collect the eggs that she had just eaten.

The sharp rap on the door came again.

She put her coat down on the bed, and going down the uncarpeted stairs she reached the hall and opened the door.

Outside to her astonishment, she saw three Gentlemen in hunting pink and behind them their horses with two grooms.

Then she saw that the Gentlemen were carrying a woman wearing a riding-habit.

'May we come in?' one of the men asked. 'Lady Barton has had a fall and hurt her arm rather badly. Yours was the first house we could find.'

Valessa opened the door further.

'Yes, of course,' she said.

The three men carried Lady Barton into the house, two lifting her at her shoulders and one at her feet.

As they crossed the hall Valessa went ahead to open the door into the Drawing-Room.

She saw then that blood was dripping down Lady Barton's hand onto the floor.

The only piece of furniture in the Drawing-Room was a very dilapidated sofa which had been put away in an out-house.

Valessa had managed to drag it into the room after all the furniture had gone.

She wanted to sit in front of the fire as she had done when her father and mother were alive and pretend that they were still there.

The Gentlemen laid Lady Barton, who had her eyes shut, down on the sofa.

One of them took out a knife and slit the sleeve of her riding-habit, which was a very smart one, up to the shoulder.

It was then easy to see that there was an ugly gash on her arm which reached from her elbow to her wrist.

'We need water and bandages!' one man said.

With a start Valessa realised that she had just been staring at Lady Barton and doing nothing.

As she hurried from the room to the kitchen she knew who Lady Barton was and had heard a great deal about her.

The village of Little Fladbury was very isolated.

It was therefore extraordinary how they always were aware of the gossip of what was happening elsewhere in the County.

The Carrier who called once a week supplied most of it.

But two of the cottagers had sons who worked in Big Houses and when they came home they had plenty to tell.

Lady Barton was, Valessa remembered as she took the kettle from the stove, enormously rich.

She had bought a huge house called Ridgeley Towers.

She had the best race-horses and the best hunters in the whole country.

Valessa had been told that she was very attractive.

Even apart from her fortune they said every eligible man in London was pursuing her.

'Yer should jus' see 'em!' the son of the Grocer in the village said when he came home. 'Loik flies roun' a 'oney-pot they be.'

Valessa had heard talk of riotous parties.

Although she had been more interested in the horses, she had been curious enough to ask why Lady Barton was so rich.

' 'Twere 'er father,' she was told. 'Made a mint o'money with 'is ships, 'e did, an' some say as it were 'cause he used 'em for collectin' slaves!'

Valessa had been shocked.

She had read denunciations of the slave traffic. And she understood that it brought in huge profits for those who were prepared to take part in it.

There was no doubt that Lady Barton entertained lavishly.

Not only was the local Hunt Ball held at Ridgeley Towers, but there were numerous other Balls.

The Grocer's son said they caused so much work that the staff were 'nearly dead on the'r feet'!

When Valessa first heard of Lady Barton she has thought she must be quite old.

Then she learnt that although she was a widow she was not yet thirty.

'She is certainly beautiful!' Valessa thought as she collected a basin.

She picked up a linen towel that was too ragged to be sold but which she had fortunately washed and hurried back to the Drawing-Room.

Lady Barton now had her eyes open and was being given brandy from a flask which one of the gentlemen was holding to her lips.

'Oh, here you are!' the man exclaimed who

had told her to fetch the water.

She put down what she was carrying and said:

'I will just go upstairs and get some linen for a bandage.'

'And something to wipe away the blood,' he said sharply.

Valessa realised he was treating her as a servant, but she thought she should expect that, seeing how shabby she looked.

She went up the stairs knowing that the only linen left in the house were the sheets on her bed.

She pulled off the top one, knowing it was something she would not need again.

She was thinking as she did so that she had already sold all the blankets except for the one on her own bed.

To keep warm she had piled on top of it some old and tattered curtains that were past repair.

She found a pair of scissors she had overlooked in a dressing-table drawer.

'They might have been exchangeable for at least an egg,' she thought.

Then she went down the stairs again.

By this time Lady Barton was talking.

'That is enough, Harry,' she said, pushing the flask to one side with her uninjured hand. 'I shall be tipsy if you give me any more!'

'All that matters is that you are alive, Sarah,' one of the men remarked.

'How can I have been such a fool as to fall at that fence?' Lady Barton asked.

Valessa reached her and realised that nothing had been done about her injured arm. They were waiting for her.

'I wonder,' she said to one of the men, 'if you would mind cutting off a piece of this sheet with which to clean Her Ladyship's arm, and then some strips for a bandage?'

He looked surprised.

She turned to kneel down beside the sofa and pour the warm water into the basin.

The man to whom she had given the sheet was just staring at it.

'Get on with it, Cyril! Make yourself useful!'

'I cannot see why I should have to do all the dirty work,' Cyril replied, 'while you give me orders!'

'If you cannot do a little thing like that for me,' Lady Barton said plaintively, 'I shall not ask you to stay again.'

'Of course I will do anything for you,' Cyril said quickly.

'And that goes for all of us,' Harry added.

Cyril cut a piece of linen the size of a handkerchief and handed it to Valessa.

'I hope this is not going to hurt,' she said

to Lady Barton, 'but I must get it clean!'

Lady Barton looked at her for the first time.

'Who are you?' she asked. 'And what are you doing in this empty house?'

'I am...leaving,' Valessa said quietly.

She started very gently to wash the gash on Lady Barton's arm who gave a little scream.

'That hurts!'

'I am sorry,' Valessa said.

'Have another drink!' Harry suggested.

'All right, anything is better than feeling pain!' Lady Barton agreed.

Harry handed her the flask and she poured a great deal of its contents down her throat.

'Dammit!' she exclaimed. 'That was a fine run for the beginning of the Season. I would miss it!'

'It is just bad luck that you fell at that particular fence,' Harry said. 'Wyndonbury took it in style!'

'He would!' Lady Barton remarked. 'I hope he broke his neck at the next!'

'Good Heavens!' the man exclaimed who had first spoken to Valessa. 'I thought that like every other woman you were worshipping at his feet.'

'That is a good way of expressing it, Roland!' Harry remarked.

'If you want to know the truth,' Lady Barton

said, 'I hate his guts!'

Valessa drew in her breath.

Lady Barton might be very rich and very attractive, but she knew her mother would have been shocked to hear a Lady swear and talk in such a vulgar manner.

Harry sat down at the other end of the sofa.

'Now what is all this about?' he asked. 'I was just saving up for a wedding-present!'

'Well you can keep your money!' Lady Barton snapped.

'But why? What has happened?' Harry asked.

'You go and ask the noble marquis, and he will give you the answer to that.'

Lady Barton seemed to almost spit out the words.

Valessa, washing the blood away from her arm as gently as she could, thought that what Lady Barton had been drinking must have been very strong.

She suspected, rightly, it was brandy.

Cyril had cut two long bandages from the sheet and now he asked:

'If you have been insulted by Wyndonbury, we will knock his head off!'

'Then knock it off!' Lady Barton said 'It is what he deserves!'

'What can he have done?' Roland enquired.

31

'I thought you two were cooing like doves together.'

Lady Barton pressed her lips together before she said as if she could not help herself:

'If you want to know the truth, and there is no reason why you should not as you are all three such close friends of mine, he told me that I was not good enough for him!'

There was a moment of stupefied silence. Then Harry said:

'What do you mean? What are you saying?'

'I suggested to His Majesty last night,' Lady Barton replied, 'that as we meant so much to each other, we might team up together.'

Roland made an exclamation of surprise, but Harry said: 'That is what I thought you would do. After all united you would have the most remarkable stable of horses in the whole country.

'That is what I thought, too,' Lady Barton said, 'and even he had to admit that my mares are better than his!'

'So what happened?' Roland asked.

'I have just told you!' Lady Barton replied. 'He said to me:

' "My dear Sarah, you are very attractive and exciting! At the same time, when I marry it has to be to somebody whom my family will consider my equal!" '

'I do not believe it!' Harry said. 'No man could talk like that!'

'Oh, yes, he could!' Cyril exclaimed.

He drew himself up as he spoke and talking in an entirely different voice he said:

'After all, you must all realise how unimportant you fellows are, and that I am a Marquis, and of great social consequence!'

The way he spoke was, Valessa was sure, a very good imitation of the man about whom they were speaking, because both Harry and Roland threw back their heads and roared with laughter.

'That is him to a "T", Cyril!' Harry exclaimed. '*I* had forgotten you were such a good impersonator!'

'Why did you not tell me he was?' Lady Barton asked.

'I never thought of it,' Harry replied. 'When he was at Eton he was always getting thrashed for taking off the Masters and making fun of the Head.'

He laughed before he went on:

'He could impersonate anybody, so that if he gave the boys an order they would think it was their House-Master speaking, and would do the most ridiculous things before they realised it was only Cyril!'

'Do the Marquis again,' Lady Barton begged.

33

Cyril straightened himself.

'What I want you fellows to understand,' he said, 'is that I only associate with common chaps like you because we are all interested in horses. Otherwise I find you distinctly inferior, and of course to me your blood is the wrong colour.'

They all laughed uproariously, and Valessa could not help smiling.

She had got Lady Barton's wound clean by now and as the laughter stopped she said to Cyril:

'Could you please cut me a piece of linen to make a pad to put over the wound under the bandage?'

'Yes, of course,' he said. 'I can see you are a very skilful Nurse.'

'I have had to look after my father on a number of occasions when he had a fall.'

'Your father kept horses?'

'One or two,' Valessa said.

She spoke in a stiff voice because she had no wish to discuss her father with these rowdy young men.

She had a feeling they would have heard of him.

It would be embarrassing for them to know that his daughter was living in an empty and obviously dilapidated house.

'I tell you what I would like,' Lady Barton said as Valessa began bandaging her arm, 'a bite of something to eat.'

There was silence and Valessa thought they were all looking at her.

'I...am very...sorry,' she said, 'but there is...nothing in the...house.'

'Why not?'

Lady Barton was staring at her and Valessa said quickly:

'Because I am...going away and I have... eaten everything...there was for...breakfast.'

She thought it was a mistake to tell the truth and yet there was nothing else she could do.

She was then aware that everybody was looking at her as if they had not noticed her before.

'You are very thin,' Lady Barton said slowly. 'Are you telling me...?'

'I have done everything I can for your arm, My Lady,' Valessa said quickly, 'and if you will excuse me, I will take this dirty water away.'

She got to her feet as she spoke and picking up the basin in which the water was red from blood, and the kettle she went from the room.

Only as she shut the door did she hear Lady Barton say:

'I have an idea! Now, listen to me, all of you...!'

CHAPTER TWO

Valessa emptied away the dirty water and put the basin down on the floor beside the sink.

Then she suddenly felt exhausted.

She sat down on the only chair that was left in the kitchen.

Beside it was a small deal table that had a broken leg and was therefore propped up on a brick.

She put her elbows on the table and her hands over her closed eyes.

Because she had hurried up and down the stairs to get the sheet for Lady Barton everything seemed to be swimming around her.

She knew it was just weakness and it flashed through her mind that she might not be able to reach the river.

She sat there for some time trying to breathe deeply, thinking as she did so that Lady Barton would soon be leaving.

She expected to hear them laughing and talking in the hall and thought that when she did she ought to show them out of the front door.

Then she asked herself why should she

trouble as she would never see any of them again.

There was a sound of footsteps and she looked up to see the man called Harry coming into the kitchen.

'I wondered what had happened to you,' he said.

'Am I...wanted?' Valessa enquired wearily.

She knew it would be an effort to rise and go back into the Drawing-Room.

Harry looked at her.

She did not realise he was taking in her pale, thin face and the expression of despair in her large eyes.

'Wait a minute,' he said.

He went out of the kitchen and she heard him crossing the hall and she thought he had opened the front door.

She wished she could go and look at their horses which she was sure were outstanding, but she was feeling too limp even to go to the window.

She had intended to watch as Lady Barton and her three friends in their pink coats departed.

To her surprise however, Harry came back into the kitchen.

He was carrying something in his hand and when he put it down on the table she saw it was a silver sandwich-box like the one her father used to carry in his saddle out hunting.

There was also a flask with a silver top which she suspected held brandy.

'I think what you need is something to eat,' Harry said.

Valessa did not reply.

She merely thought it was a strange thing to say unless he was clairvoyant, or else particularly observant.

He opened the silver box and she saw the sandwiches he had intended to eat for luncheon were untouched.

Without saying anything he walked to the dresser which was fixed to the wall and therefore could not be sold.

On it were a few plates which were all cracked and a glass which Valessa had kept.

The others had been bought by a farmer's wife for people who came to the Farm to ask for a glass of milk.

Harry put the sandwiches from his silver box onto a plate and handed it to Valessa.

'Now eat,' he said, 'while I talk to you.'

'About...what?' she questioned.

'I have something important to say,' he replied, 'and I think you should also have a drink.'

He poured some brandy into the glass and

added a little water from a jug which Valessa had left on the side of the stove.

It had been an effort to work the pump this morning which was outside in the yard.

It was rusty and got stiff when there was a frost.

She had brought in enough water to fill the kettle and some was left for her to drink now.

Having put a glass on the table he said:

'Drink a little before you start eating.'

'I...I had better not,' Valessa answered.

'Do as I tell you!' he ordered.

Because it was easier to do what he said than argue, Valessa obeyed him.

As the fiery spirit went down her throat she felt as if she came back to life.

The colour returned to her face and Harry said:

'Now, eat while I talk to you.'

There was nowhere for him to sit and he perched gingerly on the side of the table, aware that one of the legs was supported by a brick.

He seemed to have taken over and as the sandwiches looked like ambrosia from the gods, Valessa tentatively ate one.

It was filled with a pâté which she thought was the most delicious food she had tasted in a very long time.

Without even thinking about it she put out

her hand and took another.

Then feeling she was behaving in a somewhat unrestrained manner she looked up at Harry apprehensively.

'Now, let us start at the very beginning,' he said, 'and introduce ourselves. My name is Sir Harold Grantham but everybody calls me "Harry".'

'I am Valessa Chester.'

'A very pretty name!' Harry remarked. 'Now, Miss Chester, we want your help.'

'My...help?' Valessa exclaimed in surprise.

She could not imagine there was any way in which she could help the gentleman who was talking to her or Lady Barton.

'It is quite simple,' he said. 'Lady Barton is planning a special charade to amuse her guests after dinner and wants you to take part in it.'

Valessa looked at him in astonishment.

'I...I do not...understand.'

'Go on eating while I explain.'

Valessa looked down at her plate and found to her surprise that she had eaten a whole sandwich without being aware of it.

She took up another one.

'I expect as you live in the neighbourhood,' Harry was saying, 'you have heard how lavishly Her Ladyship entertains.'

'I have,' Valessa murmured.

'She always tries to think of something new and original for every party she gives.'

He made a gesture with his hand before he continued:

'It is not easy, especially when the guests all know each other and guess what is coming.'

Valessa could understand that.

'Her Ladyship has just thought,' Harry said, 'that you would be someone new they have not seen before, and it will make them curious and also interested.'

He looked at her to see if she was following what he was saying.

Valessa took a sip of the brandy before she replied:

'I understand...but I cannot think of... anything I could...do that would...amuse anybody!'

'I will tell you what to do.'

'But...what will it be?'

He smiled.

'I think it would be more fun if it was a surprise to you as well as to everybody else. All you have to do is to come back with us to the Towers.'

Valessa put what was left of the sandwich she was eating down on the plate.

'Come...back with...you?'

Then she realised she was being very stupid.

41

'Of course...I cannot do...that!'

'Why not?'

She glanced down at her shabby gown and there was no need for words.

'I understand,' Harry went on as if she had spoken, 'that as you were going away, your luggage may have gone on ahead. Therefore Lady Barton will provide you with everything you need.'

'Do...you mean...clothes?' Valessa asked rather stupidly.

'I mean very attractive, very glamorous and very fashionable gowns!' Harry said firmly.

He thought Valessa's eyes would light up as any other woman's would have done, but she merely stared at him.

Then she asked:

'Is this a...joke?'

'No, no of course not,' he said. 'How can you imagine that after you have been so kind and bandaged Lady Barton's arm she would not be very grateful?'

He thought Valessa was not convinced and continued:

'She wants to express her gratitude by having you as her guest, and she asked me to tell you something else.'

'What is that?' Valessa asked.

'If you take part in this charade which will

amuse her friends, she will give you £200.'

'£200?' Valessa repeated.

She told herself there was something very wrong!

What Lady Barton was expecting her to do must be either wicked or outrageous for her to pay so much.

Besides, how could she go to stay at the Towers looking as she did?

Perhaps Lady Barton and her friends wanted to make fun of her.

Then she suddenly realised that £200 would save her from having to drown herself.

It would enable her to get to London where she might be able to find work. Perhaps she could be a Governess or a companion.

At least there would be no immediate hurry, and she would have time to think...and live.

It all passed through her mind.

Then she was aware that Harry, watching her, seemed to understand.

'It may seem a strange request to you,' he said quietly, 'but do you not think in a way it is a sort of adventure? Without adventures, think how dull life would be!'

'But...suppose I cannot carry out...what you want...and I am a...failure?' Valessa stammered.

Harry smiled.

43

'Even if you are, you will have £200 pounds in your pocket and new clothes to wear which I can assure you, are made by the best and most expensive Dressmakers in Bond Street.'

'I just cannot believe it!'

'Oh, yes, you can!' Harry insisted. 'You are a clever girl and you know as well as I do that anything would be better than sitting alone in this empty house. And I am sure the roof leaks!'

The way he spoke made it sound so funny that Valessa gave a little laugh.

It was the first time she had laughed for a long time and it seemed odd even to herself.

'Then that is settled,' Harry said. 'All you have to do is to leave everything to me, and I will "stage-manage" you so that you will be the star of the show.'

'You...might be...very angry with...me!' Valessa said.

'I promise you I will not be that as long as you do as I tell you.'

He stood up.

'Now get yourself ready,' he said. 'I will tell the others you have agreed, and I know Lady Barton will be very grateful.'

He walked towards the door.

'When do...you want...me to...leave?' Valessa asked.

'As soon as the carriage arrives. I sent a groom to collect one as soon as Lady Barton had her fall and it should be here at any time now.'

Valessa stood up.

'I must...go to get...my coat.'

'Take the sandwiches with you, and drink the rest of the brandy!'

It was an order and Valessa knew he was testing her.

'I will do...that,' she said meekly.

She heard Harry cross the hall, go into the Drawing-Room and shut the door after him.

Picking up the sandwiches and the glass in which there was quite a lot of brandy left, she walked up the stairs.

She thought she had stepped into a dream and it could not be true.

When she reached her bedroom she saw her coat lying on the bed and remembered she had intended to wear it so that she would drown more quickly than if she went into the water without it.

'This...cannot be...true!' she said to herself.

She put the plate down beside her coat and ate another sandwich quickly, as if she was afraid they also were part of the dream and might vanish.

Because she was aware that the weakness

45

which had overcome her in the kitchen might return, she ate yet another sandwich and drank the rest of the brandy before she put on her coat.

Now she felt a warmth inside her which had not been there for a very long time and when she looked in the mirror, her cheeks were flushed.

There was only one bonnet left which had belonged to her mother.

Valessa, her father and her mother had gone to the nearby Market Town where a Horse Fair was taking place.

Her father had bought two horses which they could not really afford and the bonnet for his wife.

Elizabeth Chester had protested at the unnecessary extravagance but her husband had insisted.

'I want you to look beautiful, my darling,' he said, 'and make every other woman who looks at you jealous.'

Elizabeth laughed. Then she replied:

'They are much more likely to be jealous because I have...you.'

'Now, and for ever!' her husband answered.

Valessa thought no one could look lovelier than her mother, especially when her father said things which made her lips smile and her eyes shine.

As she put the bonnet on in front of the mirror she thought:

'If I...die before anyone...speaks to me like that...I shall miss...something which is very wonderful in...life.'

Then she looked at the old-fashioned shape of her coat and the shabby gown beneath it and knew she was asking too much!

By a miracle she had been saved from drowning herself. It would be greedy to ask for more.

'£200!' she whispered. 'But suppose I am so...incompetent they will not...give it to...me?'

Then she thought that, if nothing else, she would see Ridgeley Towers and undoubtedly have a few good meals while she was there.

Perhaps, if she was polite and pleasant to Lady Barton, she might find her a job.

Even to be a house-maid would be better than nothing.

Then below she heard the Drawing-Room door open and there was the sound of voices before Harry called up the stairs:

'Are you ready, Valessa? The carriage is here!'

'Yes...I am...ready,' Valessa replied.

She looked round her bedroom. It seemed

incredible that she should go away without taking anything with her.

But what was the point.

She had sold everything except what was too worn to be of any use, or torn beyond repair.

Hastily, because she did not want to think about it, she left the room and went down the stairs.

Lady Barton, leaning heavily on the arm of the man called Roland, was coming out of the Drawing-Room.

She was laughing and she looked very pretty as she did so.

Her deep gold hair, which Valessa was too ignorant to know owed a lot to the dye-pot, seemed to light up the dingy hall.

Cyril was walking beside her, and as he saw Valessa he said:

'Here is our heroine!'

'Now you are not to go upsetting her,' Harry said quickly: 'She is afraid she will be a failure, and you have all to be very kind to her.'

'But of course!' Lady Barton said. 'And I am looking forward to showing you my house.'

Valessa had reached the bottom of the stairs and now she was facing Lady Barton.

'Are you...quite sure...you really...want me?' she asked hesitatingly.

'Of course I want you!' Lady Barton said.

Harry stepped forward.

'Now you two girls get into the carriage,' he ordered. 'We will ride across-country, which will be quicker, and we will be there when you arrive.'

'That is a good idea!' Lady Barton said.

Roland helped her through the front door and into the luxurious carriage waiting outside.

It was drawn by two horses and there was a footman on the box.

Lady Barton sat in the centre of the back-seat, so that there would be plenty of room for her injured arm.

Valessa squeezed in on her other side.

She hoped that the movement of the carriage would not be painful for her.

'See you later, Sarah!' Harry said. 'And remember what I said to you.'

He shut the door before Lady Barton could reply and the horses moved off.

Valessa looked back at her home and felt this could not really be happening.

She was sure that if anybody from the village saw her driving with Lady Barton, they would think their eyes were deceiving them.

'Now you must tell me about yourself,' Lady Barton said charmingly. 'Harry tells me your name is Valessa.'

'Valessa Chester, My Lady.'

'As you are going to help me, there is no need for us to be formal with each other,' Lady Barton said, 'so I will call you Valessa, and you must call me Sarah.'

Valessa's eyes widened, but she did not say anything.

Lady Barton went on:

'I expect Harry has told you who he is, and the other two are Roland, who is Lord Freeman, and Cyril, who is Lord Cyril Fane.'

Valessa thought they all sounded very grand, but she definitely liked Harry, although was nervous as to what he would order her to do.'

'I have a particularly large house-party,' Lady Barton was continuing, 'becase we are having a Steeple-Chase. I know it is rather late in the year, but I arranged it as a challenge to the Marquis of Wyndonbury.'

Her voice sharpened as she said:

'He thinks he has the best jumpers in the country, while I am quite certain that mine will beat his!'

Valessa noted the name and thought this must be the Marquis they had been talking about when they were in the Drawing-Room.

He had obviously made Lady Barton angry and she thought he must be very stuck up.

She was however, more interested in the horses, and said:

50

'I have always heard that your horses were outstanding, and my father used to admire those on which he saw you out hunting.'

'It was my father who made my stables famous,' Lady Barton said complacently, 'and also made sure my race-horses won a great number of the classic races.'

She did not explain to Valessa that her father had been born in Liverpool and made his fortune there.

Frederick Wicket had then realised that the only way he could be accepted socially was to beat the sportsmen at their own game.

His father was an unimportant Solicitor, who had provided him with a good education.

He had won a Scholarship to University and gained a Degree with an iron determination that he would become a millionaire.

He had fought his way into the Shipping Industry and ingratiated himself with one of the owners who had no son.

He had on his patron's death, been left two ships with enough money to run them.

Nothing short of an earthquake could have stopped Fred Wicket after that.

By sheer will-power, as well as his brains, he bought out his opponents or made them bankrupt until he owned the biggest Fleet anywhere in the North of England.

It did not matter to him what he carried, whether it was slaves, coal or cotton, as long as it paid, his ships were there.

He was forty before he had time to think of taking a wife.

He then chose the daughter of an impoverished Squire who could hardly believe his good fortune in having such a rich son-in-law.

Fred Wicket then bought a house in Lancashire and attempted to become a country gentleman.

Strangely enough, his wife grew to love him and furthered his ambitions socially by advising him what to do.

It was through her that quite a number of people who had dismissed him as an outsider accepted him.

This was because she had made him become a race-horse owner.

Just as he had determined to have more ships than anybody else, so now Fred Wicket knew he must have better and faster horses.

It was soon impossible for anyone who raced not to know him.

It was only a question of time before he became accepted by those who had previously passed him with their noses in the air.

He was determined that his daughter should marry well.

As she was his only child it was obvious she was going to be enormously rich.

Lionel Barton had been the eldest son of a Baronet whose ancestry went back to the reign of James I.

He was not as important as Fred Wicket might have wished.

But Sarah, who was only seventeen, fell very much in love with Lionel, and her father wanted her to be happy.

Her husband came into the title just a week before he was killed in an accident and to Sarah it was a tragedy.

Fred Wicket thought philosophically that at least she had gained a title out of her marriage and he was already planning who her next husband should be.

Then, quite unexpectedly, a year after his wife had died of what the doctor called the 'wasting disease', he had a fatal heart-attack.

It was a culmination of working without ever taking a holiday.

He had concentrated fanatically on making himself an Emperor of Finance and King of Sport at the same time.

Sarah had enough of her father's determination and indomitable will-power not to mourn for too long.

As soon as she was out of black, she sold the

house in Lancashire she had never thought was smart enough for her friends in the *Beau Monde*.

First she bought a house in Berkeley Square, where she could entertain in London.

Then after searching the countryside for something really spectacular, she chose Ridgeley Towers, not only because it was the size of a Palace, but also because it was in Leicestershire.

Within five years she had made herself indispensable to the Social World who thought that racing and hunting were the only sports that mattered.

Her father's horses were already famous and she improved their breeding and their performance.

The best Hunts were in Leicestershire.

She financed lavishly the one nearest the Towers, and also contributed to several others.

It was impossible to ignore someone who had the largest Ball-Room, a private race-course, and a hundred bedrooms in which to accommodate her guests.

Fred Wicket was conveniently forgotten.

When Sarah talked about her family, it was always of her mother's relations.

Naturally she took a number of lovers.

She had grown exceedingly pretty before she

married and afterwards she developed into a Beauty.

She was not only a most attractive young woman.

She could have the smartest and the most elegant clothes, the finest and most expensive jewellery.

She could also buy every other adjunct which contributed to a woman's attraction.

Her houses were filled with the most exotic flowers that had ever been seen outside the Botanical Gardens in Kew.

She would receive her guests against a background of orchids.

Her bedroom would be decorated with hundreds, if not thousands of roses, which made it a bower for love.

The men who became her lovers found themselves in an 'Arabian Night's' dream.

From the exotic perfume that bewildered their senses to the profusion of expensive presents she gave them.

A number of them hoped to marry Sarah but she had her father's genius and caution where a business deal was concerned.

She was well aware they were as interested in her money as in herself and she was determined to have the best.

The best meant a distinguished husband in

an unassailable social position, and with an impressive title.

Too many of the men who were in Debrett were already married.

Some of the bachelors were so unprepossessing that she was too fastidious to want them in her bed.

It was not by chance that she met the Marquis of Wyndonbury.

She had seen him of course at every race-meeting but he was seldom a guest at the parties to which Sarah was invited.

The doors of the really important and selective hostesses in the *Beau Ton* were closed to her.

She had never been to Buckingham Palace.

This fact had not worried her at least not until she decided that the Marquis of Wyndonbury was the man she should marry.

But it was more difficult than she had expected to get near him.

He would take off his hat politely to her on the race course but when she tried to talk to him he seemed to slip away almost before she had opened her lips.

She asked several of her more distinguished friends to invite him to dinner when she was present.

They all seemed to have excuses saying:

'One can never rely on Wyndonbury—he is a law unto himself.'

Or they would reply evasively:

'Oh, he prefers to host his own parties, and only goes to a few chosen friends.'

Because it seemed so difficult, Sarah had became more determined than she would have been otherwise.

Like her father, although it might take a little time, she had always got everything she wanted in her life.

Finally she approached the Marquis directly, saying she had some brood mares in which she was sure he would be interested.

As it happened, her suggestion came at a time when the Marquis was looking for a new strain, both for his race-horses and his jumpers.

He did not think of Sarah as a woman, but as an owner, and invited her to luncheon, so that they could discuss their stables.

He found her charming, intelligent and very knowledgeable on a subject that was dear to his heart.

A week later when he had accepted an invitation to stay with the Earl of Stepple he found, somewhat to his surprise, that Sarah was also a guest.

He never knew that Sarah had bought her way into the party by paying the bills of the

Earl's son which amounted to over £30,000.

She was clever enough not to over-dress or to be over-bejewelled.

She made herself charming to everybody, so that by the end of the second day they were singing her praises.

The Marquis thought it was unusual to meet somebody who was so attractive and also so intelligent.

When he went to bed he was however not thinking of Sarah but of her horses.

He had fallen asleep when suddenly he was aware there was something soft and warm beside him that had not been there previously.

He turned over to investigate, then Sarah's arms were around him and her lips were on his.

Women who knew the Marquis well knew that although he appeared to be reserved, he could be an extremely ardent lover.

He was also extremely masculine, and very passionate.

He would have been inhuman if he had not accepted the favours which Sarah offered him.

After the visit to the Earl was over they had often dined alone at Sarah's house in Berkeley Square and the Marquis left as the dawn was breaking.

Because she wanted him to stay with her at the Towers, Sarah thought up a party which she was certain would please him.

She challenged him to compete in a Steeple-Chase with a team of six riders including himself against a team of her choosing.

It was an idea that appealed to him and the Marquis had a dozen of his best horses sent ahead of him to Ridgeley Towers.

He looked forward to the Steeple-Chase beside several days' hunting.

Sarah saw him arriving in a superbly built Phaeton drawn by four chestnuts that were perfectly matched.

She had felt a wave of excitement sweep over her because she was sure her goal was in sight.

'He is mine!' she said beneath her breath.

The Marquis drew his team to a standstill outside the front door and she ran eagerly down the steps to greet him.

The Marquis was undoubtedly impressed with Ridgeley Towers.

He thought it looked the size of an Army Barracks, but inside the rooms were well-proportioned.

There had been a great many innovations and improvements made since it had first been built at the beginning of the last century.

Sarah had employed architects who were already famous.

She had also been clever enough to augment

the collection of pictures which her father had left her.

Guided by what she had heard of the Royal collection she patronised the same Art Dealers.

Several of her lovers had ancestral homes, and she 'picked their brains'.

She found out from them what was correct and acceptable amongst the aristocracy, determined not to make the mistake of buying just because an object was expensive.

She had therefore accumulated a great number of pieces that the Marquis admired, and would have been prepared to have them in his own house.

Ever since she had met him Sarah had been clever enough to ask his opinion on many subjects and she bowed to his superior judgement in every particular.

Only now when they reached the stables did she say provocatively:

'I am hoping to beat you in the Steeple-Chase, but first we have a day's hunting which I hope you will enjoy.'

'I am sure I shall!' the Marquis answered.

'That is what I love about you,' Sarah said, slipping her arm through his. 'You are not blasé, like so many men, who have so much.'

'I could hardly be blasé about horses like these!' the Marquis replied, 'and you are a very lucky woman to own such superlative animals.'

'That is what I want you to say,' Sarah said in a soft voice, 'and I am very lucky to...know you!'

She hesitated before the word 'know' wondering if she was brave enough to say 'own'.

Then she thought it would be a mistake.

The Marquis had made love to her fiercely and demandingly before she left London.

Yet she had the uncomfortable feeling that when he left her he was not thinking of how soon he could see her again.

Of course, she told herself, she was wrong, he was completely infatuated with her.

But she could not be certain.

There was something about the Marquis she could not reach however much she tried.

She knew he liked a woman to be soft, gentle and pliant, so she was all those things.

She was astute enough to realise that he would hate anything vulgar, aggressive, or unrestrained.

She therefore controlled herself admirably.

Yet even in the wildest moments of passion he had never yet said: 'I love you!'

While he accepted everything she gave him as if it was his right, she did not know what his real feelings were.

Everybody had warned her that he was the

most difficult man in London.

He never talked about his love-affairs, and they took place so secretively that even the most inveterate gossips were never quite certain they knew 'all there was to know'.

But Sarah believed she was different from his other women.

Who else was so wealthy?

That did not matter to the Marquis, as he was in fact enormously rich himself.

Who else had horses like hers?

Who else could entertain so brilliantly?

Who else could command the attention of the most spoilt and fastidious men in the Clubs of St James's?

'I have everything!' Sarah told herself, 'everything except a husband, and that place is waiting for him!'

She had been extremely careful as to whom she had asked to this house-party.

The majority of guests were of course men, who either were bachelors or accepted without bringing their wives.

Naturally, they wanted women to amuse them and Sarah had chosen Ladies who were almost as 'blue-blooded' as the Marquis himself.

She was determined he should not think that her parties were vulgar, or in any way outrageous.

What she had to convince him was that she would make him a perfect wife.

A wife who would keep him amused and happy in bed and in public was what he would expect from the Marchioness of Wyndonbury.

She had chosen her clothes with this in view.

She was not only a model of elegance and beauty, but ladylike and by no means fantastic.

Her jewels were mostly perfect pearls of inestimable value and she used less make-up on her cheeks and lips than she usually did.

She only hoped the Marquis noticed.

When she was sitting at the end of her dinner table she willed him to think how she would grace *his* table when she was his wife.

The first night after his arrival he had come to her bedroom.

She was certain then that she had won the race and the winning-post was within sight.

The dinner had been superlative.

The wine was so unusual that almost every man in the party had congratulated her on her cellar.

The conversation, too, she thought, had been exactly what the Marquis would enjoy and she had been careful not to appear too imtimate when they were with other people.

In fact, she had left the other women to fawn on him.

When he had come to her after everybody had retired, she had held out her arms with a little cry of delight.

The room was filled with orchids for which she had scoured the country.

They were white with just a touch of pink in each of their delicate petals.

Orchids have no perfume.

The carpet had been sprinkled very discreetly with the essence of white violets.

The Marquis had never seen Sarah's bed at the Towers and it had been specially designed for her.

The headboard was in the shape of a huge silver shell in which nestled a few huge pearls of real mother-of-pearl.

Curtains fell from another shell fixed to the ceiling. They were of net shimmering with tiny diamanté which caught the light.

Her pillows were edged with the finest lace.

The cover on the bed was of lace in which diamanté and pearls were embroidered into the material.

Lights were discreetly hidden behind the flowers and Sarah made a picture which would make any man gasp in admiration.

There was a faint smile on the Marquis's rather hard lips as he walked towards her.

He was wearing a long robe of royal blue,

frogged with black braid which made him appear as if he was fully dressed.

He stood looking at her as she held out her white arms.

He then became aware that apart from a single row of black pearls around her neck, she was wearing nothing else.

'I feel I am somewhat over-dressed!' he said with a hint of amusement in his voice.

Then he took off his robe...

CHAPTER THREE

The Marquis left the commotion and excitement of the kill and turning his horse he started to ride back.

He thought it was the best day's hunting he had enjoyed for a long time.

The weather had been fine, not too cold, and he knew the huntsmen and the hounds were outstanding.

He reached the nearest road which bordered the fields in which he had been riding.

He was not surprised to see a row of carriages drawing up accompanied by grooms to take over the riders' horses.

He thought that Sarah certainly did things in style.

He did not wait for anybody else and as soon as he was seated in the carriage the coachman drove off.

The Marquis thought it was a relief not to have to ride back for several miles when it was growing colder.

It was also a joy not to have anyone with him with whom he would be expected to make conversation.

He wanted to think about the Steeple-chase tomorrow and decide which of his riders should ride the horses he had brought to Ridgeley Towers.

The men he had chosen to represent what was called on the programme the 'Wyndonbury Team' were all outstanding riders.

Two of them had won classic races riding as amateurs on their own horses.

At the same time he was aware that Sarah's team was as good as his.

Harry Grantham, for example, was a first class rider to hounds, and Lord Freeman was an expert at jumping.

It was an intriguing contest, the Marquis thought then he remembered what he thought had been a very difficult moment last night.

He had made love to Sarah in her exotic and sensational bedroom and had just been thinking it was time he returned to his own.

Then with her head on his shoulder she said very softly:

'I think, Stafford, darling, we should not only join our stables together, which would be fantastic, but also we should join ourselves.'

For a moment, because he was sleepy, the Marquis did not take in what she was saying.

Then she murmured beguilingly:

67

'I would make you an exemplary wife and no one could be a more handsome or exciting husband!'

The Marquis could not believe his ears.

It had never struck him for one moment in his *affaire* with Sarah that she might be wanting marriage.

He knew a great number of men had pursued her.

He had thought somewhat scornfully that they were fortune-hunters who would find it impossible to ignore a widow who was wealthy.

But marriage was something which at the moment did not figure in his scheme of things.

He wanted to be free to enjoy himself.

He was quite aware, as his family continually reminded him, that sooner or later he must have an heir.

He was determined it should be 'later'.

He had not yet reached his thirty-third birthday and it could be at least five or six years before it became a serious problem.

He was well aware there was no young woman in the Social World who would not accept him eagerly.

His position at court as well as his ancestry which was one of the oldest in England made him almost unique.

He was extremely proud of his Family-Tree.

The Wyndonburys had played their part in every reign after one had been knighted at the Battle of Agincourt.

An ancestor had been an adviser to Queen Elizabeth, another had been a close friend of Charles II, and almost as much a Roué as he was.

The Marquis knew that his ancestral home was one of the finest examples of Elizabethan architecture still in existence.

His Picture Gallery was filled with the portraits of his predecessors.

They had been painted by all the greatest artists of the day and perhaps those by Van Dyck were the most outstanding.

The Marquis had learned the history of each one of them and he could say proudly:

'None of my family has ever made a *mésalliance*. My father used to boast that our blood was as blue as that of any King who ever sat on the English throne.'

It had never struck him that he would not carry on the tradition, when the time came for him to take a wife.

He had been approached by quite a number of the aristocracy.

The Duke of Cumbria only two months ago had suggested in a somewhat embarras--sed manner that he had three daughters of marriageable age.

'There is no one,' he said, 'I would welcome more warmly into my family than you, Wyndonbury.'

The Marquis had managed to refuse the offer without offending the Duke.

He made it clear that he had no intention of being married for a long time.

He took good care not to go to Balls or parties where the host had an unmarried daughter.

He certainly ignored any debutante who happened by chance to be in a house where he was a guest.

He was astonished that Sarah Barton, whose father came from Liverpool, should suggest being his wife. It had left him speechless.

Because he was tired his brain was not as alert as it usually was and he therefore said the first words that came into his mind.

'My dear Sarah, you are very attractive, and very exciting! At the same time, when I marry, it has to be to somebody whom my family will consider my equal!'

After he had spoken, Sarah was very quiet, and he thought a little belatedly that he might have worded his rejection of her more charmingly.

Because he had no wish for her to be hurt, he kissed her, and thought in fact that she was quite happy before he finally left her.

Because he had only seen her this morning when they were mounting their horses for the Meet, he wondered if she was annoyed with him.

Then he told himself she could not have been serious.

How could she think that he would marry somebody who, to put it bluntly, was not of his class?

He was well aware because she was so rich that Sarah had been accepted by a great number of the *Beau Monde*.

They could not resist the parties she gave or her generosity to those she considered her friends.

He also knew that many hostesses at whose houses he was always welcome would not allow Sarah to cross the threshold.

'These people with new money,' one Dowager snorted in his presence, 'should stay where they belong!'

The Marquis looked at her for explanation, and she said:

'I am talking about that Barton woman. I have heard that her father made his money out of shipping those wretched negroes out of Africa and selling them as slaves!'

The Marquis had not been aware of this

71

before but he asked:

'Are you certain these stories are true? People are often unkind about heiresses, especially when they are also good-looking!'

'I can assure you I had it from a most impeccable source,' the Dowager answered. 'In fact, if you are curious, it was the Chancellor of the Exchequer who told me!'

There could be no argument about that and as the Marquis did not wish to discuss Sarah he moved away.

Then when one or two other people said almost the same thing to him he knew it was the truth.

He did not pretend however that he did not find Sarah amusing.

He was too clever not to be aware that she was deliberately restraining herself when he was with her.

She did not flaunt her money, as she was inclined to do in front of other people.

He found the luxury of the way she lived almost overwhelming.

The flowers, the fruit, the wine, the food were only part of it. In his opinion there were too many footmen wearing an ostentatious livery.

There were too many embroidered and lace-edged sheets and pillow cases made of a fine linen.

What was more, he thought, the carpets were unnecessarily soft, and he could say the same about the beds.

He appreciated, because she was so rich, that Sarah wanted the best.

Yet like all people without a long line of ancestors behind them, she continually overstepped the mark.

One thing he was not prepared to criticise was her horses.

Her stable was at least the equal of his and he was not certain that one or two of her racehorses were not better.

Because she had made herself so knowledgable on the 'Sport of Kings', he enjoyed talking to her.

He had come to stay at Ridgeley Towers quite simply because he could not resist seeing Sarah's racing stable.

He also wanted to inspect the mares of which she had told him so much.

But marriage—that was a very different thing!

He thought he could understand however the way she had reasoned it out that their combined stables could be a sensation.

Because she was a woman, it seemed logical to her that they too should be joined together.

73

However that Sarah should be the Marchioness of Wyndonbury was unthinkable.

He found her passionately very satisfying, but he thought of her in the same way as he did of an exceedingly alluring actress who had been his mistress last year.

That also applied to a lovely little ballet-dancer from Covent Garden whom he had enticed away from Harry Grantham, much to his annoyance.

She had been French and had a fascination and a *joie de vivre* which he had never found in an Englishwoman.

She had been under his protection for nearly nine months.

He had then said good-bye, giving her an expensive present which she added to her jewellery which was the envy of the whole cast, and they had parted amicably.

At least that was what the Marquis wanted to believe.

Sometimes however his conscience pricked him, because when he left a woman to whom he had made love he was aware that she had not only given him her body, but also her heart.

It was something he always regretted because he himself had never been in love.

He had been told often enough how painful it could be.

But he often wondered why he had to suffer tears, recriminations and undoubted misery when he ended an *affaire*.

He hoped apprehensively he would not have to go through the same dramatics where Sarah was concerned.

'I will leave the day after tomorrow,' he told himself.

He knew Sarah was expecting him to stay for another two days' hunting.

He decided he would leave early after breakfast, which would enable him to reach London in plently of time for dinner.

This was possible because on his way to the Towers he had arranged for four changes of his own horses to be ready on his way back.

He wondered if Sarah would repeat her proposal of marriage.

Then he told himself he had made it abundantly clear that he would not marry her.

She was too intelligent to labour the point.

Nevertheless he felt slightly anxious when he reached the Towers.

Only as the carriage drew up did he realise that he had not seen Sarah since early in the morning.

He thought it rather strange.

As he walked into the ornate hall he saw Harry Grantham coming down the curved, carved and gilt staircase.

'Did you have a good day?' Harry asked genially.

'What happened to you?' the Marquis enquired.

He realised that besides not seeing Sarah he had not seen Harry or his boon companion Cyril Fane.

'Sarah had a fall,' Harry explained.

'A fall?' the Marquis repeated. 'Good Lord! Is she all right?'

'She has injured her arm a little and is resting, but you will see her at dinner.'

'What bad luck!' the Marquis said. 'She missed an excellent day's sport, and so did you.'

'I know,' Harry said regretfully, 'and I cannot help feeling envious, but that is something you have made me feel before.'

The Marquis laughed lightly.

'You will have a chance to even with me tomorrow,' he said. 'They are betting it will be either you or me who will win the Steeple-Chase.'

'I will certainly do my damnedest to beat you,' Harry replied.

The Marquis laughed again and walked up the stairs to his bed-room.

He had no idea that Harry was not joking,

but actively hating him.

He had never forgiven the Marquis for taking away Yvonne, and he had sworn to himself that one day he would get even with him.

Now he had the chance, and he was determined not to miss it.

Lying in her glittering silver and pearl bed, Sarah asked her Lady's-maid who was taking away her tea-tray:

'Is Miss Chester all right?'

'She's asleep, M'Lady,' the maid replied. 'I peeps in about ten minutes ago to ask her if she'd like some tea, but she were sleepin' like a child, and I thought it better to leave her alone.'

'That was sensible,' Sarah approved. 'Sir Harold said she must have a glass of milk as soon as she is awake, and anything else she wants.'

'I've put one by her bed, M'Lady.'

Harry had been so explicit with his orders that Sarah had let him have his own way.

When they had arrived back at the Towers, on Harry's instructions they had immediately had luncheon.

There had been just the five of them and they had eaten in a small Dining-Room which was exquisitely decorated but at the same time cosy.

Valessa therefore did not feel so embarrassed by her appearance as she would have otherwise.

The three men certainly went out of their way to put her at ease.

By the time she had eaten a little though it seemed to her to be an enormous amount, she was laughing.

Although she did not know it, she was looking extremely attractive as she did so.

Then Harry sent her upstairs to bed.

Sarah had gone with her and she was shown into the most beautiful room she had ever seen.

It had a painted ceiling, a bed draped with satin curtains, several pieces of French furniture and an Aubusson carpet on the floor.

'Now you are not to worry about anything!' Sarah said. 'Just leave Harry to produce you as a star to amuse and intrigue our party.'

'I wish you would...tell me what I...have to...do,' Valessa asked tentatively.

'That would spoil the surprise,' Sarah said. 'When I have rung for the maid to help you into bed, I want you to let my Seamstress take your measurements so that she can alter the gowns I have for you, and I know you will look very pretty in them.'

Valessa thought this was impossible, as she was so thin and weak.

At the same time, although she had not managed to eat much of the delicious dishes at lucheon, she felt better than she had for a long time.

Sarah had summoned the Seamstress.

When they were alone before she arrived she gave Valessa an envelope.

'There is no need to open it,' she said, 'you know what it contains.'

Valessa blushed.

'I...I feel I should not...take so...much.'

'You will find you have earned it when you do as Harry wants,' Sarah said enigmatically. 'And I have promised you some very beautiful clothes.'

The Seamstress took Valessa's measurements and when she had gone the maid helped Valessa to undress.

Wearing a diaphanous nightgown which she supposed belonged to Sarah, Valessa got into bed.

It was more comfortable than anything she had ever slept in and she was very aware of the lace that trimmed the sheets and pillow cases.

The cover, which was also of lace was, she was sure, very valuable and ought to be behind glass.

There was so much she wanted to explore in the room.

She had already seen in a small mahogany book-case books bound in red leather and embossed with gold.

But when her head was on the pillow, she realised how tired she was.

Even before the maid had finished tidying the room she was asleep.

Valessa was woken by the sound of someone moving about.

She realised when she opened her eyes that the curtains were drawn, the candles lit, and two maids were arranging her bath in front of the fire.

Valessa watched them for a moment and the maid who had helped her before came to the bed-side to say: 'There's a glass of milk here for you, Miss, which I were told you'd to drink as soon as you woke.'

Valessa was sure that it was one of Harry's instructions, and she obediently sat up and drank the milk.

She thought there was something else in the glass which she suspected was a touch of brandy.

It made her feel better.

Then when the bath was ready the maids poured in hot and cold water from large brass cans which she knew were placed outside the room by a footman.

She had heard his voice when she got out of bed.

The bath was scented with a delicious perfume which she could not identify.

The warm water seemed to wash away her sleepiness and also a lot of her apprehension as to what she was expected to do.

She dried herself with a bath-towel which had been warmed in front of the fire, then the maid brought her a chemise of the finest silk trimmed with real lace.

There was a long slip also of silk to go under her gown.

To her surprise, it fitted her exactly.

She decided the Seamstress must be very experienced to be so precise after simply taking her measurements.

The gown that went over the slip was of white gauze and was trimmed round the hem and on the sleeves with rows of lace and bunches of rose buds.

Tiny diamanté drops nestled in each flower as if they were drops of dew and the lace round her neck was sprinkled with them.

The sash which encircled her tiny waist was of pink with a large bow at the back.

Valessa thought it was the most beautiful gown she had ever seen.

An elderly maid who she learned waited on Sarah came to arrange her hair.

It was swept away from her forehead and fell into curls at the back of her head.

The elderly maid patted a little powder on her face, a touch of rouge to her cheeks, and a little salve to her lips.

Valessa was aware that Ladies in London used cosmetics, but her mother had left her face untouched.

She had never expected to be powdered and painted.

For a moment she wanted to protest, then she remembered the cheque that was in the top drawer of her dressing-table.

Unless she was to give the money back she must do exactly as she was told.

She had to admit that by the time the maids had finished with her the result was fabulous.

She wondered if she was expected to go downstairs, and was just about to ask when there was a knock on the door.

When the maid opened it, she heard Harry's voice say:

'I want to speak to Miss Chester. Ask her to go into the *Boudoir* next door.'

The maid curtsied, then she showed Valessa what she had not noticed was another door near the window.

When it opened she found herself in a *Boudoir* that was as luxurious as her bed-room, filled with the fragrance of flowers.

Harry was waiting for her.

As she walked towards him hoping for his approval, she thought he looked very impressive in his evening clothes.

He was not wearing knee-breeches, but long drainpipe trousers.

They had been introduced, her father had told her, by the late King George IV when he was Prince Regent.

Valessa walked nervously until she reached Harry.

Then she looked up at him pleadingly. He smiled and said:

'I would never have recognised you as the same girl I found sitting so despondently at the kitchen-table!'

Valessa laughed, because it was not what she had expected him to say.

'Do I look...all right?'

'You look lovely, as you must have seen for yourself in the mirror,' he answered.

He glanced over his shoulder to see if the communicating door was shut.

Then he said:

'Now listen, Valessa, the charade in which you are acting will take place to-morrow evening. To-night, I want you to enjoy yourself just as one of the guests. But go to bed early, for I am sure you will want to watch the Steeple-Chase.'

Valessa's eyes lit up.

'Can I do that?'

'Of course,' he said, 'and I hope you will be willing me to win.'

'Of course I shall!' Valessa said fervently.

'Now, do not be nervous,' Harry said. 'Just make yourself charming to whoever is sitting next to you at dinner, and be very evasive if anyone asks you where you have come from.'

'What shall I say?' Valessa enquired.

'That you live in the country, seldom go to London, and are very fond of horses!'

'That is true.'

'Then talk about them,' Harry said, 'or rather, let everybody else talk while you listen.'

'I will...try to do what you...tell me.'

'Stop looking worried,' Harry commanded. 'Act as if you are enjoying yourself!'

'I am sure...I shall,' Valessa replied.

Then she gave a little laugh.

'How could I do anything else when I am here in this magnificent house and wearing a gown which could only have come from my dreams?'

'That is exactly what I want you to feel,'

Harry said. 'Now, come along, Sarah is waiting for you.'

He took Valessa along the passage.

At the top of the stairs Sarah was standing looking lovely, Valessa thought. She wore a gown of emerald green that seemed to be almost transparent.

There was a necklace of emeralds around her neck and a tiara on her golden head.

As they joined her Valessa was aware that Sarah was looking her over almost as if she was trying to find fault.

Finally she said with a smile.

'Perfect! That gown might have been designed for you.'

She looked at Harry as she spoke who said:

'That is what I thought!'

They went down the stairs, Sarah leading the way.

Two footmen hurried to fling open the doors to what Valessa learned later was called 'The French Salon'.

Sarah swept in.

For a moment all Valessa could see were the chandeliers lit with hundreds of candles and a kaleidoscope of people, some of the men in pink evening-coats.

The women were as exquisite as stars in silks and satins, all glittering with jewels from their heads to their feet.

To Valessa's surprise, Sarah put her arm around her and drew her towards them saying:

'I want to introduce you to an old friend of mine—Valessa Chester—who is as knowledgeable about horses as any of you, she will cheer on my team tomorrow and make sure we are the winners!'

There was laughter at that.

Then Lord Cyril Fane and Lord Freeman came up to shake Valessa by the hand.

She was sure they had been told to do so by Harry.

She was introduced to quite a number of other men.

They went into the Banqueting Hall and she realised there were forty people sitting down at the table which was laden with gold ornaments.

For the first time in her life, and Valessa was sure it would be the last, she ate off gold plate.

Although the food was delicious she was intent on what was happening around her, feeling it could not be real, and was just a part of her imagination.

She obeyed Harry's instructions, and talked about horses.

'Have you any horses of your own, Miss Chester?' one of her dinner partners asked.

'My father had, and I rode almost before I could walk!'

He laughed at that.

Then he was telling her how old he was when he first rode, after which they talked of the competition to-morrow.

'Wyndonbury will be the winner!' he said. 'He invariably gets everything he wants in life!'

'I should have thought that was bad for him,' Valessa said, and her partner laughed.

Then because he had mentioned the Marquis she looked for him down the table.

She had been too nervous before dinner to look around, merely concentrating on anybody who was speaking to her.

Then she saw him, seated on Sarah's right.

He was, she thought, exactly as she had expected and thought she could have picked him out in any crowd as being the most important man present.

There was something very authoritative about him.

It was even more obvious than the fact that he was exceedingly handsome.

His features, she told herself, were aristocratic and if she had not known he was a Marquis, she might even have thought he was a King.

She smiled, and the man on the other side of her asked:

'What do you find amusing?'

'My own thoughts,' Valessa replied.

'Now you are making me curious,' her partner said, 'and who is the lucky man about whom you are thinking?'

'Actually, I was thinking of the Marquis.'

'A great many people think about him,' was the reply, 'and the annoying thing is, invariably the lady I am with!'

The way he spoke made Valessa laugh.

'I have just been hearing what a success he is,' she said.

'He must have been born under a lucky star!' her partner replied. 'But as I often tell myself, there is no use being envious or jealous of a man like that!'

Valessa thought this over, then she said:

'I think that is a good way to think of people who are out of reach and whom it is impossible for us to emulate.'

'My advice to you, Miss Chester, is not to fall in love with Stafford Wyndonbury!'

'I was not thinking of falling in love,' Valessa answered, 'but of course you are right, and it would be a tragedy for anyone to love "The Man in the Moon"!'

'That is a very apt description of him,' her

partner said, 'and that is what I shall always call Wyndonbury in the future—"The Man in the Moon"!'

When dinner ended Sarah led the ladies from the room.

When they reached The French Salon where they had assembled before dinner, in a voice only she could hear she said to Valessa:

'Slip off to bed now without saying good-night to anybody. Harry wants you to have a good night's sleep and feel really well to-morrow when there will be a lot to do.'

Valessa did as she was told although because she felt better she would have liked to stay.

She had the feeling that she must savour every moment of this strange and unexpected adventure.

Harry had been right—that was exactly what it was!

When it came to an end she knew she would want to remember everything that had happened.

As she reached her bed-room, she felt some of the excitement ebbing away and she knew Harry was sensible.

She was tired, and she was weak.

Two meals and a short sleep were not enough to give her back her health and buoyancy she had when her father and mother were alive.

A maid was waiting to help her undress and when Valessa was in bed she put a cup and saucer and a jug beside her.

'That's milk, Miss,' she said, 'and if you wakes in th' night, you're to drink as much as you can.'

Also by the bed was a pretty box which Valessa was told contained biscuits.

'There's every sort in there if you gets hungry, Miss,' the maid explained.

'I have just eaten a large dinner!' Valessa smiled.

'If you wake you may feel peckish,' the maid answered. 'I often does meself!'

She looked around the room to see that she had remembered everything.

'Good-night, Miss,' she said, 'an' sleep well!'

As she shut the door Valessa lay back for a moment against her lace-trimmed pillows.

It was true! She was here and she was being maided, cosseted and fed like a prize turkey.

For what?

That was the question she could not help feeling was repeating itself over and over again in her mind.

What did all this mean?

Why should the rich Lady Barton suddenly wish to entertain her?

Why should she provide her with beautiful

gowns, and Sir Harry Grantham take so much trouble over her?

Suddenly none of it seemed to matter.

Whatever she had to do she could not believe it was anything very terrible.

There was £200 in the drawer of her dressing-table and she had been promised more gowns like the one she had worn this evening.

'I am so lucky, so very, very lucky!'

Then with what was almost a rapt note in her voice she said:

'Thank You...God...thank You!'

Downstairs in the Salon several people spoke to Sarah about her friend.

'She is very attractive, Sarah! Why is it we have not met her before?' Lady Mortlake asked.

'She lives in the country,' Sarah explained, 'and actually, she has been ill, which is why she has gone to rest after her journey here.'

When the Gentlemen joined the ladies there was cards for those who wanted to play.

Music came softly behind a screen of exotic blossoms which hid the musicians.

The Marquis played cards until midnight, then he rose from the table and said he was going to bed.

He would have left the room without saying

good-night, if Sarah had not intercepted him.

'You are turning in early, Stafford?'

It was a question, and her eyes looking up at him were very revealing.

'I need to have my wits about me to-morrow,' he replied.

She put out her hand and he gallantly, and at the same time gracefully for such a large man, raised it to his lips.

'Will you come and say good-night to me?' she asked in a whisper that only he could hear.

He shook his head.

'I really am tired,' he said, 'and you know the reason why!'

She gave him a dazzling smile and her fingers tightened on his.

'I shall miss...you.'

'If you are sensible,' he replied, 'after having a fall you will go to bed early. Does your arm hurt you?'

'A little!'

'Take care of yourself.'

His tone was sympathetic.

He left the Drawing-Room and walked up-stairs.

As he did so he thought with satisfaction that Sarah was sensible enough not to be upset or to take umbrage because he had said he would not marry her.

'It must have been just a passing idea,' he told himself confidently. 'She could not really expect me to accept her as my wife!'

His valet was waiting for him, and when he was undressed and in bed, the man said:

'We're all betting on Your Lordship bein' the winner ter-morrow.'

'I hope I shall not disappoint you,' the Marquis replied.

'There isn't much likelihood of that, M'Lord! You always wins!'

It was a statement of fact.

Although the Marquis had heard it a thousand times before, it pleased him.

As he shut his eyes he was thinking of the Steeple-Chase.

He was quite confident that his team would win the expensive Gold Cup which Sarah had promised as a prize.

CHAPTER FOUR

Driving towards the race-course, Valessa felt wildly excited.

She had always longed to see a Steeple-Chase and although her father had ridden in several, she had not accompanied him.

She had heard that the Steeple-Chases arranged by Lady Barton were more demanding and more professional than any others in the County.

After she had seen Ridgeley Towers, she was prepared to believe it.

She had been told by the maid who called her that she should be downstairs by ten-thirty.

When she reached the hall she found it filled with people.

There were men in pink coats collecting their hats and gloves from the footmen, seven of them wore peacock blue, which she discovered had been provided by Sarah for her own team.

They looked very smart with velvet collars, white revers and white cuffs.

She noticed however that the Marquis seemed to be regarding them disdainfully.

He, as she had expected, looked outstanding wearing the pink coat of his own Pack and his boots appeared more brightly polished than anybody else's.

The teams mounted their horses, and there was a long row of carriages for the spectators.

Valessa was told she was to travel with Sarah.

When she got into the carriage she found that Lord Cyril Fane was seated opposite them.

'Are you not riding?' she asked in surprise.

'Sarah does not consider I am good enough!' he said with a wry twist to his lips.

'You are a very good rider, Cyril!' Sarah said. 'It is simply that I had to choose seven and I think, if you are honest, you will admit that each one of them is exceptional.'

'Nevertheless, I am humiliated!' Lord Cyril said.

But he was smiling as he spoke and Sarah replied:

'You will have your hour of glory tonight.'

They exchanged glances.

Valessa wondered a little nervously if it had anything to do with the charade in which she had to take part.

She knew however she should not ask questions.

Actually she was content to look about her.

The Park with its old oak-trees was very

attractive as they drove through it.

Then when she saw the race-course she knew it was everything she expected, and more.

It was laid out on a flat piece of land beyond which there was an incline up to a thick wood.

The jumps were, Lord Cyril told her, the highest in any Steeple-Chase he had ever known or heard of.

To Valessa they seemed enormous and she wondered if any horse would be strong enough to jump them.

It was then she saw that the Marquis had mounted and knew her fears were groundless.

She had expected him to ride a superb horse.

His stallion which was being obstreperous was the most outstanding animal she could possibly imagine.

It obviously had Arab blood in it, and she did not only admire the horse, but equally its rider.

Then there was a great deal of preparation, instructions from the referees, and a long wait while the teams got into line.

Valessa found herself watching the Marquis.

She knew that just as he had stood out in the Dining-Room on the the race-course there was no one to touch him.

She had promised Harry that she would

will him to victory.

But she found it impossible to look at any of the riders except the Marquis.

He was riding with ease and what appeared to be a lack of effort.

This was different from many of the other men who seemed somehow insignificant beside him.

She had so often watched her father and had attended some Point-to-Points and Horse Fairs with him.

But Valessa knew the Marquis was as exceptional as if he was a god from another Planet.

'Or perhaps,' she thought with a little smile to herself, 'the Man in the Moon!'

He was holding his stallion on a tight rein.

At the same time keeping ahead of the other riders, to make sure there was no obstruction when he came to a fence.

He took the first in style, although it seemed exceptionally high.

The stallion seemed to fly over the second and third jumps.

Then Harry was riding beside him and Valessa had the feeling there was no one else in the race.

They certainly were doing their utmost.

The pace and the way the horses took the jumps was, she thought, breathtaking.

The Steeple-Chase was four times round the course, then there was a long run up to the winning-post a quarter-of-a-mile away.

'It is not usually used,' Sarah told her.

They watched from the starting-point the riders going round three times.

Then Sarah ordered the coachman to take them to the winning-post.

Because it was so exciting, Valessa found it impossible to listen to anything Sarah and Lord Cyril were saying.

She just found herself watching the Marquis and because he was such an outstanding rider, she knew that she wanted him to win.

The carriage drew up at the winning-post.

Looking back they could see the Marquis and Harry were taking the last fence still side by side.

The rest of the field was nearly two lengths behind them and Valessa realised this was the crucial moment.

She found it hard to breathe as the two riders came galloping towards them.

They seemed to be equally matched and the horse on which Sarah had mounted Harry was nearly as fine as the Marquis's.

Nose to nose they drew nearer and nearer.

Then Valessa realised that by a superb piece of riding the Marquis passed the winning-post a head in front of Harry.

They had been watched at the Winning Post by a number of the other guests who cheered wildly.

Valessa could only clasp her hands together and wish her father was with her.

Then she heard Sarah say almost beneath her breath:

'Damn him! I wanted Harry to win!'

'He rode extremely well!' Lord Cyril said.

'Not well enough!' Sarah retorted sharply.

'Never mind,' Lord Cyril said, 'he will have his revenge!'

'That is true,' Sarah agreed, and now she was smiling again.

The two riders, having pulled in their horses, came back towards them.

The rest of the field had by now passed the winning-post and they also were turning back.

The Marquis and Harry reached the carriage first.

'That was the most exciting race!' Sarah said. 'Bad luck, Harry! But you did your best!'

Lord Cyril was talking to the Marquis.

'Congratulations!' he said. 'And if you want to sell that horse at any time, I will buy it!'

'I would not part with *Saladin* for all the money in the world!' the Marquis replied.

He bent forward to pat the stallion's neck

and there was an expression on his face which made Valessa feel that after all he was human.

Then laughing and talking, the Marquis receiving a great number of congratulations, they rode back to the house.

There were nearly a hundred people at luncheon because a number of neighbours had come to watch the race.

As it finished Sarah presented the Marquis with a magnificent gold cup.

'I feel,' she said, 'that this is "coals to Newcastle" but of course I give it with my warmest congratulations and an admiration which I cannot put into words.'

She looked at the Marquis as she spoke.

Valessa had the feeling however it was not admiration she had felt for him but the anger which Sarah had expressed when she was bandaging her arm.

Then as the Marquis took the cup she saw him smile at her.

'I am sure I am wrong. They have made up their row, and she is no longer angry with him,' she thought.

As they left the Dining-Room Harry caught hold of her arm and said in a voice that only she could hear:

'Go and lie down. I want you to look your

best this evening.'

Valessa drew in her breath.

She had heard there was going to be an exhibition of jumping during the afternoon, and she longed to see it.

But there was a firmness about the way Harry spoke which made what he said an order.

Everybody else went out through the front door to mount their horses or waited for their carriage which left Valessa alone to walk up the stairs.

When however she got into bed, she knew Harry had been sensible.

She still felt a little weak.

But a large breakfast, the milk she drank before she went to the race-course, and an excellent luncheon had made her feel more like her former self.

Yet she was wise enough to know that if she was to please Harry this evening she would need to have her wits about her.

She must certainly avoid the exhaustion she had felt before.

Her maid drew the blinds and closed the curtains.

Five minutes later, Valessa was asleep.

When she next awoke, Valessa was to find a delicious tea had been placed beside her.

There were hot scones, sandwiches, and cream cakes.

She wanted to laugh because it was not only a case of 'rags to riches', but from 'fasting to a feast'.

'I am very, very lucky,' she told herself for the thousandth time.

She wanted to move, but she felt it more sensible to rest, and she even dozed a little before the maids brought in her bath.

Again there was a beautiful evening-gown for her to wear.

This time it was very pale green and decorated with white camellias.

There were two real camellias to wear in her hair, and when she went downstairs, Harry looked at her with approval.

For the first time, she actually spoke to the Marquis.

He was standing beside Sarah who put out her hand to check Valessa as she walked past them.

'Come and tell the Marquis what you thought of the Steeple-Chase, Valessa,' she said.

'I have never watched anything that was so exciting!' Valessa exclaimed.

'I was just telling our hostess how much I enjoyed myself!' the Marquis said.

'Your horse is magnificent!' Valessa went

on. 'And you were...'

She stopped, thinking perhaps she sounded rather over-effusive.

'And I was—what?' the Marquis enquired.

'There are no words...appropriate to express such...superb riding,' Valessa answered.

'Thank you!' the Marquis said.

'My father used to say,' Valessa went on, 'that no man can be a good rider unless he is part of his horse, and his horse is part of him!'

She made a little gesture with her hands as she said:

'But that does not really explain it.'

'I know exactly what you are trying to say,' the Marquis replied. 'I have never heard it expressed exactly in that way.'

Valessa wanted to go on talking to him.

But Harry came up to her with an elderly man she had not talked to before.

Dinner was announced, and again it was as excellent in every particular as it had been the night before.

After the enormous number of guests at luncheon, Valessa was not surprised to find there was just the house-party.

It seemed to her that the men were more noisy and laughing more frequently than they had the previous evening.

She wondered if it had anything to do with the wine.

She noticed that the servants re-filled every glass as soon as anyone took even a sip from it.

She was very careful to drink only a very little champagne.

She knew that in her weak state alcohol of any sort would go to her head.

'I must keep my brain clear for what I have to do,' she told herself.

Then once again the question was there— what was it to be?

Would it be anything she found frightening?

When the ladies left the room she felt sure the time when she had to 'sing for her supper' had come.

She remembered her old Nanny saying:

'You never get anything for nothing in this world!' and she was sure it was true.

She had received more than she had expected, and now she would have to pay for it.

Before they reached the hall Sarah said very quietly:

'Go upstairs! My maid Hannah is waiting to dress you.'

Valessa felt her heart give a frightened leap and without saying anything she walked up the stairs to her bedroom.

Hannah, the elderly maid who had done her

hair, was in her bedroom.

'Now you've got to change, Miss,' she said.

'I cannot believe you have anything for me as pretty as the gown I have on!' Valessa replied.

Hannah unbuttoned it, and as she did so Valessa was aware that there was a gown and several other things lying on the bed.

They were all white.

What Hannah now slipped over her head was another beautiful gown that was different from the others she had worn.

It reached the floor, and there was a small train billowing out at the back.

It was also not so *décolletée* as the gown she had worn at dinner.

It was certainly very beautiful and was trimmed with lace and white satin ribbons which Valessa was sure had come from France.

Hannah made her sit down at the dressing-table and arranged her hair in a different style from how she had worn it at dinner.

Then she put more powder on her face and slightly more salve on her lips.

Valessa thought she had finished.

Hannah went to the bed and came back with something in her hands.

It was a long lace veil and when she draped it over Valessa's head she asked in surprise:

105

'Surely this is a wedding-veil?'

'It's wot Her Ladyship wore at her own wedding,' Hannah replied.

'B.but...why...?' Valessa began.

Then she felt it was a mistake to ask questions of the maid.

Harry had said he was producing this charade, and she expected that Hannah did not know any more than she did.

There was a wreath of orange blossom to hold the veil in place, and Hannah arranged it so that it covered her face.

Valessa was rather glad that she could look at the world, or rather the audience, without their being able to see her clearly.

There were long white kid gloves to wear, but Hannah did not cover her left hand, just buttoned it at the wrist.

Lastly Hannah gave her a bouquet of white roses and lilies-of-the-valley which Valessa thought was very lovely.

All this took some time, but she was ready when there was a knock on the door.

Hannah opened it and Harry came into the room.

'Wait outside, Hannah!' he said.

The maid went into the corridor and closed the door behind her.

Harry walked to where Valessa was sitting

in front of the mirror.

'You look marvellous!' he said. 'Just as I wanted you to.'

'What is it...I have to...do?'

'Now listen, Valessa,' he said, 'we have a joke to play on our friends, and a competition which they have to guess.'

Valessa was listening and she raised her face to his and was looking at him through her veil.

'What I have staged,' Harry went on, 'is a wedding which will take place in the Chapel.'

Valessa had noted there was a Chapel in the house and because the building was old it was something she thought she might have expected.

'You will be a bride,' Harry was saying, 'but the bridegroom will be in a wheel-chair, so the congregation will not be able to see him clearly. He will also wear dark glasses.'

He paused for a moment as if he expected her to ask a question.

When she said nothing he went on:

'All those in the Chapel will see is you coming up the aisle on my arm, and the bridegroom's back. They are supplied with cards on which they have to write the name of who they think he is. Those who get it right will receive one of Sarah's expensive prizes!'

He smiled as he spoke as if it was a joke.

Valessa thought it was an original idea.

'Now come along,' Harry said, 'and do not feel nervous.'

'I am sure I shall be...all right,' Valessa replied.

'All you have to do is to make your responses in exactly the same way as you would in a real wedding. Afterwards Sarah has thought up a special surprise for you!'

'She has been so kind to me already,' Valessa said, 'that I could not take...any more!'

'Nonsense!' Harry exclaimed. 'One can never have too much of a good thing. Come along, I expect they are ready for us now.'

Valessa rose to her feet.

She thought she would not be frightened if she could hold on to Harry's arm and it was certainly an original idea to amuse a house-party.

Harry took her down the stairs and through the hall.

They walked a long way down a corridor which Valessa thought must lead to the back of the great house.

She suspected that it was the old part and when she reached the Chapel she was sure she was right.

All the house-party were already inside, sitting in the ancient carved pews.

Valessa could see through her veil that they were laughing and talking to each other, but in whispers because the organ was playing.

The Chapel was quite small and beautifully decorated with white flowers.

The only light came from six candles on the altar.

What made it different from an ordinary service was that the front pews were covered with lilies which made a barrier between the congregation and the bride and bridegroom.

Valessa thought it was a clever idea so as to hide the latter and make it more difficult to identify him.

As she and Harry reached the door, the organ played 'Here Comes the Bride'.

They proceeded up the aisle to where Valessa saw a Clergyman was standing waiting for them.

She supposed he was an actor, and he certainly looked the part.

He was an old man with white hair and a beard, and she had a feeling she had seen him somewhere before.

Then she told herself that if he was an actor, that was impossible.

Because she was playing a part she kept her head slightly bowed as she thought a bride would do.

She could however see out of the corners of her eyes the laughing faces of the guests as they scrutinised her.

She and Harry passed through the barrier of lilies.

Now, as they stood in front of the clergyman, Lord Cyril pushed a man in a wheel-chair into the Chapel from the Vestry door.

He was wearing a pair of dark glasses, and yet as Valessa glanced at him without turning her head, she was aware it was the Marquis.

He was sitting down rather low in the wheel-chair, his hands clasped in front of him.

She thought that as they could not see his face it would be very difficult for those in the congregation to identify him over the barrier of lilies.

She realised too that the Chapel, except for the altar, was very dark.

As the Marquis was drawn up beside her the Clergyman started the Service.

'Dearly Beloved, we are gathered together here today...'

Valessa had heard it so often in their little village Church. Her mother had always made a point of accepting invitations to the weddings of the village girls, and had taken her with her.

Twice when she had been young she had been a bride's-maid, first to the Vicar's

110

daughter, then to the Doctor's.

She thought it would be easy for her to repeat every word of the Service.

Then the Parson said to the Marquis:

'Say after me: "I, Stafford Frederick Alexander, take thee, Valessa..."'

The Marquis repeated the words in his very distinctive voice that would certainly be a clue to those listening.

Then it was her turn.

'I, Valessa, take thee, Stafford Frederick Alexander, to my wedded husband...'

She spoke without a pause.

A wedding-ring was produced and the Marquis with the aid of Lord Cyril who guided his hand, placed the ring on her finger.

It was rather small and she had the idea that it was Lord Cyril who finally ensured it was in its right place.

Then they knelt and the Clergyman blessed them.

It was only then that Valessa thought it was wrong to make a mockery of what was a Sacrament of the Church.

She had prayed so often that she would be blessed.

She felt that a blessing by a Priest, which she had always thought came from God Himself, should not be imitated by actors.

The Service ended.

She wondered if she would be expected to go down the aisle beside the Marquis in his chair or perhaps he would rise to his feet and take off his spectacles.

Her question, which she could not put into words, was answered.

Lord Cyril pushed the Marquis past the altar and out of the Chapel again through another door.

Valessa followed him.

She was glad that they were not to continue play acting in what was a consecrated building.

She was sure her mother would have been shocked.

She expected now they were all going to the Salon and the 'congregation' would receive their prizes there.

Outside the Chapel they passed a staircase which she suspected led up to the First Floor.

But they went a little further and turned into a Sitting-Room which like everything else in the house, was furnished in a luxurious fashion.

There was only a candelabrum with three candles alight in it.

There were some decanters and glasses on a table, and as Lord Cyril pushed the Marquis near to it, Sarah said:

'Do not take off your disguise. We want the others to see you close up, and we must give them time to move from the Church back into the Salon.'

'Yes, of course,' the Marquis replied.

'And you certainly deserve a drink,' Lord Cyril remarked, 'for the splendid way in which you have acted your part.'

He poured some wine into a small glass as Harry said: 'And that equally goes for Valessa! She was absolutely fantastic!'

'Of course she was!' Lord Cyril said. 'Give her a drink. She deserves it!'

'No...I am all...right,' Valessa smiled.

'Rubbish!' Harry said. 'You have a long evening in front of you, and as your Stage Manager I insist you drink to your success.'

She laughed.

Lord Cyril was bending over the Marquis and Harry was standing in front of her with a glass in his hand.

She put down her bouquet, lifted her veil with both hands and threw it back over her wreath.

Harry handed her a liqueur.

At least she thought that was what it was.

'Now drink all of it,' he said, 'or I shall be angry! It will make you feel marvellous, and ready to receive all the compliments that are due to you.'

As she took the glass in her hands she heard the Marquis say:

'Your good health, Valessa, and may you always be happy!'

'Now you must drink to him!' Harry said in a low voice.

'Yes...yes...of course,' Valessa agreed.

She lifted her glass.

'To you, My Lord, and of course to *Saladin!*'

She tried to see the Marquis as she spoke, but Lord Cyril was standing in the way.

'Now that was a very good toast!' Harry exclaimed. 'Drink up!'

Because she wanted to please him Valessa did as she was told.

She felt the liqueur which was very sweet slipping down her throat.

'It...tastes very...nice...' she began to say.

Then suddenly she felt she must sit down.

A chair was behind her and she lowered herself into it.

She felt as if the room was moving round her.

She gave a little gasp and reached out her hand as if to support herself.

Then she knew no more...

Valessa felt that she was at the end of a very long, dark tunnel with just a glimmer of light at the end of it.

It seemed to waver and beckon to her and she tried to move towards it.

Suddenly there was the sound of laughter, and people were talking.

She was not certain what they were saying.

She could hear them and thought it was a nuisance when she wanted to be quiet and sleep.

The light was getting brighter, and the voices louder.

'Wake up, Valessa! Wake up!'

It was a woman's voice speaking to her.

Although her eye-lids felt as if they were weighed down with lead, Valessa opened her eyes.

She saw Sarah's face, and it was above her.

The laughter seemed to be accentuated until it was so loud that she felt it hurt her ears.

'Wake up!' Sarah ordered.

A man's voice was saying the same thing, but he was speaking to somebody else.

Sarah's face became clearer until it came into focus.

Valessa could see the diamond tiara she was wearing on her head, and the huge necklace of diamonds that was round her neck.

'Wake up, Valessa,' Sarah said again, 'and meet your bridegroom!'

It was then that Valessa remembered the charade.

She supposed now they were going to give out the prizes to the people who had guessed who the bridegroom was.

Suddenly she was aware that she was lying down and it seemed strange!

She wanted to sit up. Sarah moved aside so that a man she thought was Lord Freeman could put his arm behind her.

He pulled her up against some soft pillows.

As he did so she realised that somebody beside her was being lifted in the same way.

Slowly she turned her head which felt stiff, and saw it was the Marquis.

He was no longer wearing his dark glasses, and his eyes were opening slowly.

Then Valessa was aware that the whole house-party was standing round the end of the bed laughing and making jokes to each other about them.

She felt a little wave of resentment seep through her.

Then she heard the Marquis say:

'What the Devil's—going on? What is—all this—about?'

'We are celebrating your marriage!' Sarah replied. 'And you have certainly been hasty in taking your bride to bed!'

There was something in the way she spoke which made Valessa wince.

'I do not know—what your are—talking about,' the Marquis said, 'or why I am—here!'

He made a movement as if he would get off the bed. Then he put his hand up to his forehead.

'What—have you—given me?' he asked angrily.

'Just a pleasant little drug,' Harry replied, 'which made you do exactly what we wanted. You will feel better when you have had something to drink.'

He held out a glass to the Marquis, who pushed it away.

'What are you—talking about?' he demanded.

Harry turned so that the guests could hear what he said:

'Now let me explain—we had a competition in which you all had to guess the identity of the bridegroom. It was of course, the Noble Marquis!'

He looked at him, then went on:

'You all saw him, slightly disguised and in a wheel-chair, marry Miss Valessa Chester in the Chapel.'

'I guessed who he was!' someone listening exclaimed.

'So did I!' another voice chimed in.

'It was not really difficult,' Harry said, 'and of course you will all receive prizes. But what you did not realise, and this is the whole joke of the evening, the Marriage Service was genuine and the Parson an ordained Priest! What is more, Sarah has a Marriage Certificate to prove that the elusive Marquis has been caught at last!'

For a moment there was a stupefied silence.

Then as Sarah held up triumphantly what Valessa saw was a Marriage Certificate, the men began to laugh.

They laughed uproariously.

Valessa was certain that most of them were drunk.

Then the Marquis, with what Valessa felt was a tremendous effort, flung his legs off the bed and stood up.

'This joke had gone too far!' he said in a cold voice.

'It is no joke,' Sarah said. 'It is true. You had a Special Licence signed by the Archbishop of Canterbury! And this is your Marriage Certificate! You are married, Stafford! Married to a girl whom I picked up yesterday in rags and suffering from starvation in a house that was empty of every piece of furniture!'

She spat the words at him. At the same time,

there was a note of venom in her voice that was unmistakable.

The Marquis looked across the bed at her.

'How can you have done such a thing?' he asked.

'I did it to teach you a lesson!' Sarah answered. 'I was not good enough for you! Well, I hope you enjoy yourself with a wife whose blood is not blue, but more like the water from a sewer!'

For a second after she had spoken there was silence.

Then the men were laughing again, and the sound seemed to echo and re-echo round the room.

'Get out! Get out, all of you!' the Marquis said.

He did not raise his voice, but it was unmistakably an order.

For a moment nobody moved. Then Valessa saw some of the ladies who had been at the back of the room turn towards the door.

The Marquis stood waiting, seeming in a strange way overpowering, dwarfing and dominating everybody else in the room.

Finally there was only Harry and Sarah left.

'You too, Grantham!' the Marquis said. 'Get out before I strike you!'

'You took Yvonne from me,' Harry answered, 'and I can only tell you that you deserve all you get!'

'And that,' Sarah interposed, 'is a wife who, whether you like it or not, is now the Marchioness of Wyndonbury!'

She threw the Marriage Certificate she had been holding in her hand down on the bed.

Then she too, a little unsteadily, walked towards the door.

'God Bless the Bride and Groom!' she said mockingly. 'And may you both rot in hell!'

She went with Harry from the room, slamming the door behind her.

Valessa listening felt that she was turned to stone.

This could not be happening! It was a nightmare from which she would wake up.

Yet at the back of her mind she had the terrifying feeling that it was true.

She felt her heart beating because she was so afraid.

Her mouth was so dry that she could hardly open her lips and it was then she realised she had been drugged.

The Marquis walked across the room to stand with his back to the fireplace.

Valessa realised he was looking at her and she shivered.

She wondered frantically what she could say.

How could she explain to him that she did not know what was happening?

Suddenly, as if he made up his mind, he said harshly:

'Go and get ready. We will leave here as soon as it is light!'

CHAPTER FIVE

As the Marquis finished speaking he walked slowly and with dignity from the room.

He did not look back at Valessa but she felt the vibrations of his anger emanating towards her like a tidal wave.

She felt as if her head was filled with cotton-wool and her legs were not her own but very slowly she managed to get off the bed.

As she did she looked down at the Marriage Certificate where Sarah had thrown it, and thought it could not be true.

Sarah had said that a Special Licence had been signed by the Archbishop of Canterbury and the Clergyman who had married them was genuine.

Valessa felt herself shiver.

Then when she managed to reach the door she found herself in the corridor where her bedroom was situated.

There was nobody about although she could hear a number of people laughing and talking downstairs.

When she reached her room she found there

was no maid waiting for her but to her surprise, she saw a large trunk by the wardrobe.

The trunk was open, and she could see the gowns that Sarah had given her had already been packed.

She thought with horror how every detail of this degrading charade had been thought out.

They had anticipated that the Marquis would leave as soon as possible and because they were married, he would have to take her with him.

She wanted to refuse, to run away.

But she thought if she did so, he might perhaps force her in front of the servants to obey him.

It was difficult to think or to plan what she should do.

She looked at the clock on the mantelpiece and saw that it was not yet two o'clock in the morning.

This meant if the Marquis wished to leave when it was light she would have to wait for over four hours.

She felt utterly and completely exhausted.

It was difficult to walk, let alone think, so she undressed and got into bed.

The milk that had been left for her the previous night was on a table by the bedside.

When she had drunk some of it, her throat did not feel so dry. But she knew the drug was making her stupid.

She fell asleep almost at once.

It seemed only a few minutes before the maid's voice beside her said:

'It's six o'clock, Miss, an' 'Is Lordship wishes to leave in half-an-hour.'

For a moment Valessa could not understand what was happening.

Then she remembered.

'I must get up,' she said, speaking more to herself than to the maid.

'I've brought you some breakfast, Miss. You'll feel better after you've had a cup of coffee.'

Valessa had the idea that the maid thought she had drunk too much the night before.

Then she saw the white gown lying crumpled on the floor where she had thrown it, she could understand what the woman was thinking.

Somehow it did not seem to matter.

All she wanted was to get away and never see Harry Grantham or Sarah Barton again, who had tricked her as well as the Marquis.

As she forced herself to eat her breakfast and drink her coffee she was thinking that what had happened could not be legal.

But she had the terrifying feeling that it was.

Surely, even Sarah could not have faked a Special Licence and a Marriage Certificate.

Then as she drank a little more of the coffee, she held her breath.

The Parson who had signed it had written '*J Rowlandson*', and she remembered who he was.

He was the Vicar of Ridgeley where the Towers was situated.

Once when their own Rector was ill he had come to their village to take the Service on Sunday.

He had been a younger man then, and his hair was not white as it had been last night.

But that was why, Valessa now realised, she had thought she had seen him before.

'It is true! It is true!' the jeering voice of the men who had laughed at them last night seemed to be repeating.

She had the terrifying feeling they might be waiting downstairs to laugh and jeer at her again.

The maid was at the wardrobe taking down the clothes that had been left for her to wear.

Valessa saw there was a warm gown and to wear over it was a thick coat trimmed with fur.

Because they were Sarah's she wanted to refuse to put them on.

But there was no sign of the gown and coat in which she had arrived and she told herself she would be foolish to leave without the trunk.

125

She suddenly remembered the envelope containing the money that Sarah had promised her.

She looked in the drawer of the dressing-table and for one moment of horror realised it was not there.

Then the maid who had buttoned up her gown said:

'Her Ladyship tells me to pack everythin' when you'd gone down to dinner last night, and I puts the letter that was in that drawer in your bag.'

There was a satin reticule on one of the chairs.

Valessa thought with a feeling of relief that at least she would be independent of the Marquis.

She would ask him to take her home, or perhaps to a Posting Inn where she could hire a carriage.

Anything would be better than having to be embroiled with Sarah Barton.

She remembered the spiteful way she had spoken last night.

Her rudeness and the look of venom that had been in her eyes as she glared at the Marquis.

'She is common and she is horrible!' Valessa thought. 'I hope I never see her again.'

The maid brought her an attractive bonnet which matched her coat and as she was putting

126

it on there was a knock on the door.

When the maid opened it a man's voice asked:

'Is the trunk ready?'

'Yes, it is,' the maid answered, 'but you'll 'ave to strap it up for me, Mr Bowers.'

'That's all right.'

He walked into the room, saw Valessa and said:

''Morning, Miss! 'Is Lordship wants to get off as soon as you're ready. The 'orses are comin' round now from th' stables.'

'I am...ready.' She had the idea that the man was the Marquis's valet.

As he had picked up the trunk and was carrying it outside the maid said:

'There's a bonnet-box, too, Mr Bowers and don't you forget it!'

'I won't,' Bowers replied.

There was obviously a footman in the corridor waiting to help him.

Valessa had heard another man's voice speaking outside.

Then as they must have moved away she gave a last glance at herself in the mirror and saw she was very pale.

There were also dark lines under her eyes which she thought must have come from the drug that had been given her.

'Goodbye!' she said to the maid. 'I am...
sorry I have no...money with which to thank
you...but actually...as you have very likely
...guessed I have not a...penny to my...name!'

'That's all right, Miss,' the maid replied,
'and Good Luck! Wherever you're goin'!'

Valessa thought she would need it, but she
did not say so.

She hurried down the Grand Staircase aware
as she did so that her legs still felt a little
strange.

The Marquis was in the hall, one footman
helping him into his over-coat, another handing
him his high hat and gloves.

To Valessa's relief there was no sign of
anybody else.

She only hoped that they had drunk far too
much last night to be aware of what was happening this morning.

The Marquis's Phaeton was waiting outside.

Although Valessa was not aware of it, the
Marquis had designed it for himself for travelling.

Unlike most Phaetons, it had room for the
luggage underneath the high seat at the back
which was intended for the groom.

He preferred to have his valet travel with
him.

The man was there when he arrived and he

did not have to wait for a Brake.

This for other travellers carried the servants and the luggage from place to place.

His grooms travelled with him as out-riders.

Valessa noticed there were two of them waiting beside the Phaeton, mounted on superb horses.

One of them was *Saladin*.

A footman helped her in while the Marquis got in on the other side.

A thick fur-lined rug was placed over her knees.

She thought as there had been a frost last night and the sun had not yet risen it was very cold.

The Marquis drove off.

Only when they had gone a short distance down the drive did Valessa say in a small, hesitating voice:

'Would it...be possible for you...?'

Before she could say any more, the Marquis, without turning his head said:

'Be silent! I have no wish to speak to you until we reach London!'

The note of cold authority in his voice made her conscious of how very angry he was.

She looked at him without revealing that she was doing so.

She knew by the squareness of his chin and

the tightness of his lips that he was forcing himself to be self-controlled.

She moved as far away from him as she could, squeezing herself against the side of the Phaeton.

The seat was heavily padded and was very comfortable.

She felt nevertheless as if she sat on a table of nails.

She wanted to tell him it was not her fault, that she had been deceived just as he had.

But he had told her to be silent.

She wondered how long that silence would have to last.

The Marquis was calculating that Ridgeley Towers was eighty miles from London.

He remembered that many years ago the Prince of Wales, later George IV had broken the record driving to Brighton.

His Royal Highness had driven 53 miles in 5½ hours.

The Marquis was certain that with his horses he could do better.

That was what he had planned yesterday when he had decided to leave promptly after breakfast and arrive in London in time for dinner.

Now he determined to get to London as quickly as possible.

Then he had another plan to put into operation, but he had no intention of discussing it with the woman who was sitting beside him.

How was it possible, he asked himself, that he could have been tricked in such an outrageous manner?

He had thought, perhaps conceitedly, that Sarah loved him.

It was what invariably happened when he had an *affaire de coeur* with one of the Beauties.

Now he knew what had happened was in fact, his own fault.

Sarah had certainly not been suitable from the point of view of breeding, nor for that matter, in character, to be his wife.

But she was not a 'Cyprian' or 'Bit o' muslin'.

They could be paid off when he was no longer interested.

Sarah wanted marriage. She therefore considered herself to be intolerably insulted that he didn't think her good enough to be the Marchioness of Wyndonbury.

Any other woman would, he knew, have wept on his shoulder.

She would have let him see how unhappy he had made her, but ultimately of course, she would have accepted the inevitable.

Sarah had too much of her father in her.

Fred Wicket had, as the Marquis knew, fought like a tiger to reach the top of the tree, oblivious of whom he annihilated on the way up.

Sarah had wanted to annihilate him socially, and he thought she had undoubtedly succeeded.

He had barely noticed this creature who was now his wife when he had spoken to her last night.

Now he could hardly remember what she looked like, except she had been very thin, if well dressed.

If Sarah was right and she came from the gutter, what could he do about it?

He would see the faces of his relations when they learnt that he, whom they had begged and pleaded to marry, had now a wife.

She doubtless spoke with a Cockney accent.

She however, would be triumphant, he thought despairingly, as Sarah had been last night when she had held up the Marriage Certificate.

Then her face, which he had thought so attractive, had been grotesquely ugly as she had jeered at him spitefully.

'Your wife who, whether you like it or not, is the Marchioness of Wyndonbury.'

He could hear the laughter of the men staring at him from the foot of the bed.

He could see an expression which he thought was one of shock, as well as surprise, in the eyes of the women behind them.

He could imagine how the story would be repeated and repeated all over London.

In the Drawing-Rooms and Boudoirs of his friends, the Clubs of St James's and of course in Buckingham Palace where the King and Queen would not be amused.

The Marquis was intelligent enough to know that he had been successful for too long.

Quite a number of people, even those who habitually accepted his hospitality, would be glad to see him knocked off his pedestal.

His horses had been too frequently first past the Winning Post.

He had captured the hearts of too many beautiful women.

He had taken away a pretty 'Cyprian', as in the case of Harry, in whom another man had been interested.

Of course he knew there must be people who were both envious and jealous.

He would be pilloried as a fool who had been tricked into having a woman from the gutter foisted on him when he was too drugged to be aware of what was happening.

It was humiliating enough to realise that he

had been unconscious while he was being married.

He remembered now how after the ladies had left the room the port was passed round the table.

After twenty minutes the men had followed.

Harry, who was taking it upon himself to play the host, had said:

'Wait a minute, Wyndonbury! Sarah asked me to offer you a glass of a very special port which is more mature than anything we have been drinking so far.'

'I really think I have had enough,' the Marquis remembered saying.

'I should have thought of it earlier,' Harry said, 'but give it a try because if you like it Sarah has a case for you, and she thought you might like to give one to His Majesty.'

The Marquis was well aware that the King was always prepared to receive a present.

He was quite certain that anything Sarah bought would be extremely expensive and also very good.

He had therefore let Harry pour the port into another glass.

He had sipped it and thought it had 'body' and was different from the rather light port he had been drinking before.

'What do you think?' Harry asked.

He had taken two more sips.

Then as he considered what he should say, he felt the room going dark and remembered nothing more.

'How could I have anticipated that Grantham would behave like that?' he asked himself.

It was hard to believe that because he had taken Yvonne away from him Harry had been plotting and scheming to have his revenge.

As the Marquis drove on he felt the sound of the horses' hoofs and the wheels as they turned seemed to be asking the same thing:

'What are you going to do about this woman? What can you do?'.

At first Valessa found the tremendous speed at which they were travelling was exhilarating.

She had never moved so fast before.

She was aware that the Marquis drove as well as he rode, and with an expertise she had never seen before.

She knew how her father would have enjoyed driving these perfectly matched chestnuts.

Just as he would have been entranced by the movement of *Saladin* whom she could see galloping in the field beside them.

The groom on him was a good rider.

But Valessa could not forget how magnificent the Marquis had been when he took the jumps in the Steeple-Chase.

'At least I shall have that to remember,' she thought.

Then she began to plan that when she could speak to the Marquis she would tell him that she would go back to the country and live in her own home.

If she was very careful with the money Sarah had given her, she would be able to refurnish her bedroom and the Sitting-Room.

Then she would have enough left over to last for some time.

She would keep out of his way.

Perhaps later, if he did not wish her to starve, he would give her a small allowance.

If not, she would go to London.

Because she was so used to telling herself stories, she found herself going over every detail of what she would do.

She believed there were Domestic Bureaux where she could find what sort of positions were available.

She was sure she could teach young children, although perhaps she looked too young.

She had a feeling that Governesses were usually women of middle-age.

Perhaps she could be a companion to an old lady, but again she might be too young.

'You will have to help me, Mama,' she

said in her heart.

Then, almost as if she had forgotten his existence, she glanced at the Marquis.

He was her husband!

She was married to him, and the only way they could be legally separated would be by a divorce which would have to go through the Houses of Parliament.

She did not have to imagine how much the Marquis would loathe the scandal, the gossip and the reports in the newspapers.

She knew it would be horrifying for him and degrading for her.

She remembered her father saying once:

'No Lady should appear in the newspapers, except for when she is born, when she marries, and when she dies!'

'What can I do, Papa?' she asked.

There was no answer.

The Marquis drove his horses for twenty miles.

Then he drew in at a Posting Inn where his own horses were waiting to change over.

He said sharply to Valessa:

'You have fifteen minutes, and do not keep me waiting!'

Bowers helped her down from the Phaeton.

As she went into the Inn a maid in a mobcap took her upstairs to a bedroom where she could wash and tidy herself.

She thought it was a long time since she had had breakfast and was just about to ask for food when it was brought to her room on a tray.

There were cold meats and a glass of champagne.

Valessa was wise enough to realise that food was essential unless she was to collapse.

She was certain that would make the Marquis even more angry than he was already.

She sipped a little of the champagne and found it gave her an appetite.

It was difficult however to eat very much of the meats, but she managed as much as she could.

When Bowers knocked on the door to tell her that the Marquis was ready to leave, she finished the champagne.

They set off again, this time with a team of bays to draw them.

She sat back in the Phaeton and shut her eyes.

Then she realised he was taking her to London she knew it would be a very long journey.

She was afraid she might feel again the terrible exhaustion she had experienced before she left home.

'I must not be too tired,' she told herself, 'so

that when we arrive I cannot talk to him about the future.'

She was aware when they reached the next Inn where they were to change horses that she was feeling tired.

Once again there was food, but here it was better than it had been the first time.

This was because an out-rider had been sent ahead across country.

He had got there before them and alerted the proprietor.

There was warm soup and roast chicken for Valessa and she could have had a choice of apple-pie or cheese, but she found it impossible to eat any more.

She had however enjoyed a cup of steaming black coffee which she thought would keep her awake.

Then they were off again.

Now, because there was a faint drizzle of rain, the hood of the Phaeton had been put up.

There was also a hood over Bowers at the back.

Because they were enclosed, the Marquis seemed to be nearer and more intimidating than he had been before.

It was frightening, Valessa thought, to be shut up in what was almost like a cave with a man who would not speak to her.

She could still feel his hatred and his disgust vibrating towards her.

She hoped that perhaps when she told him she was not as lowly born as Sarah had said she was, he would be relieved.

That was, if she ever had the chance to speak to him.

It seemed ridiculous that they could travel together for so many hours without exchanging a single word.

And yet she was far too frightened, after the way he had told her to be silent, to speak again.

They drove on and on, and because Valessa was aware how her father travelled, she knew it would take four changes of horses before they reached London.

She was aware that the Marquis was too experienced a driver to push his team.

But he kept up a fast, even pace, and she suspected that he was trying to beat a record.

On and on they went.

When they reached the fourth and what she thought must be the last change, Valessa was half asleep.

So it was agonising to have to get down from the Phaeton and walk into the Inn.

The food was ready, and again there was soup, a generous portion of salmon and some roast lamb.

She managed to eat the soup, a few mouth-fuls of the salmon, but that was all.

There had been champagne at all the places they had stopped.

Now there was a bottle of claret on the tray and the maid who brought it in explained:

'We ain't got no champagne for 'Is Lordship, only a red wine.'

'Thank you,' Valessa replied.

Normally she would have drunk nothing, but she knew her strength was waning.

She hoped that the claret would keep her go-ing until they arrived at their destination.

She had felt rather cold during the last part of the journey, so she kept as close as she could to the fire.

She warmed her hands before she put on her gloves which were too smart and too tight-fitting.

'I must keep...them under the...rug,' she told herself.

If was an effort to go down the twisting oak stairs from the bedroom into the hall and out to where the Phaeton was waiting.

Again it was Bowers who helped her in.

She noted, because she loved horses, that the Phaeton was now drawn by a jet-black team.

Each horse had a white star on its nose, and a white front fetlock.

She sat down and pulled the rug up until it covered her chest.

The food and wine had warmed her and she felt sleepy. She had the idea however, that it was not just ordinary tiredness she was feeling.

The utter exhaustion she had been afraid of was now threatening to engulf her.

'I must...reach London...without being... tiresome,' she told herself desperately.

She felt somehow as if her whole body was disintegrating.

Even if she had wanted to raise her hands, it would be an impossibility.

'If I can go to sleep,' she thought, 'then perhaps when I wake I will be able to talk to His Lordship.'

It was difficult to put her head against the hood of the Phaeton, because she was wearing a bonnet, so she undid the ribbons and took it off.

She wondered if she should explain to the Marquis why she did so.

Then as she glanced at him she was aware that he was looking even grimmer than he had before.

'He is...hating me! He is...hating...me!' she told herself, and shivered because she was frightened.

She put her bonnet down on the seat beside her.

Because she was so thin and had moved as far away from the Marquis as she possibly could, there was a wide space between them.

Then she pulled the rug even higher, shutting her eyes, as she rested her head against the cushioned back.

She felt as if waves of exhaustion were making her feel disembodied.

She was sinking into a strange oblivion which was dark, frightening, and there was no one to save her.

Then she knew no more...

Valessa turned over and thought she was back in bed at home.

She supposed she should go downstairs and pump some water that she could heat for her breakfast.

'The fire!'

The words seemed to spring into her mind.

She had forgotten the fire. Perhaps, the one in her bedroom had gone out in which case she would be unable to light the one in the kitchen.

She was aware that she was moving.

It was then she remembered that the Marquis was driving to London and she thought

143

he was taking a long time to get there.

'I must talk to him when we arrive,' she told herself, and knew it would be a tremendous effort.

'I am...tired...I am so...very...tired!' she whispered.

She opened her eyes, then thought she must be dreaming.

She was in what seemed to be a very small room, but there was movement, and she could not think why.

'I must be...giddy? Perhaps it was the... claret I...drank at the last place we...stopped!'

Then she was aware that the movement was not that of wheels and that she was in bed.

In bed and, although it seemed impossible and absolutely incredible, she was in a ship.

She tried to sit up, but it was too much effort. She lay and looked up at the ceiling that was not very high above her.

It was then she saw there were two port-holes in her cabin.

There were some pretty, expensive-looking curtains drawn over them and the rocking of the ship made them move so that the sunshine could be seen beneath them.

'Where...am I? What is...happening?' Valessa asked.

She was afraid.

The Marquis must have been determined to be rid of her so he was sending her away.

But where to?

She lay trembling as different ideas kept flashing through her mind.

Now she could hear the slap of the sails and the creak of the timbers.

There were also footsteps as if somebody was moving about on the deck above her.

'Where...am I? What is...happening?' Valessa asked again and she was very frightened.

The cabin-door which was opposite the bed, opened very quietly and slowly. She drew in her breath.

Then she saw a man's head peeping in at her and realised it was Bowers.

'Are you all right, M'Lady?' he asked cheerily.

'Where...am...I?' Valessa enquired.

Her voice did not sound like her own, but was very small and hesitating.

Bowers came into the cabin and shut the door behind him.

'I thought you'd never wake up,' he said, 'but now you have, I s'pose it's a bit of a shock!'

'Where...am I?' Valessa asked.

'You're aboard 'Is Lordship's yacht the *Ulysses*.'

'A...yacht!'

Because she was so astonished she sat up in bed.

Then she glanced down at herself and saw she was wearing the silk chemise trimmed with lace which she had put on under her travelling-gown.

As if he knew what she was thinking, Bowers explained.

'You passed out, M'Lady, when we reached London, an' we couldn't wake you, so 'Is Lordship brought you along, just as you were, so to speak.'

'Brought me along...where?' Valessa asked trying to understand.

'The *Ulysses* were anchored in the Thames, just past the 'Ouses of Parliament,' Bowers explained.

Valessa was looking at him wide-eyed, as he went on:

'So we just stops to pick up a few things from Berkeley Square and comes straight on 'ere and was out to sea 'fore it were dark!'

Bowers made it sound almost like an adventure story, and Valessa asked tentatively:

'Where...are we...going?'

'You'll 'ave to ask 'Is Lordship. On the bridge he be now, talkin' t'the captain, but I can't hear wot they're saying.'

Bowers grinned at her, then he said:

'Now wot you wants, M'Lady, is somethin' nice to eat, and if you take my advice you'll stay where you are 'til we're in calmer waters.'

He reached the cabin-door as he spoke, and as he opened it he said:

'If Your Ladyship wants a wash, there's a bathroom on yer port side.'

Then he was gone and Valessa stared after him in astonishment.

How could she have slept or been unconscious, when His Lordship had reached London and brought her away in his yacht?

She supposed when she thought about it that he was running away from Sarah and all those horrible laughing, jeering people who had clustered at the foot of the bed.

She could see them only too clearly, their flushed faces and open mouths mocking them.

She did not need to be told how humiliating it was for the Marquis.

She had wished that the earth would open up and swallow her.

Why had she not known instinctively that what she was doing was wrong and refused to take the part that had been assigned to her?

She knew the answer only too well.

She had either to agree to what Harry proposed to her, or else find her way to the river.

Anyway, there was no use thinking now what she should have done.

It had happened, she was here in this yacht with a strange man who hated her.

Because she thought it would make her feel a little better she struggled to the door on the port-side that Bowers had indicated and to her astonishment found it was in fact, a bathroom.

Valessa had heard about bathrooms, but this was the first time she had actually seen one.

Her mother and father had always bathed in their bedrooms, as she had done.

But when she was alone in the house she was far too tired to carry water up the stairs.

She had then put the bath as near as possible to the kitchen-door that led into the yard.

She had pumped the water into a can that was not too heavy for her to carry.

She had taken it into the house and poured it into the bath.

She had not been over-generous with the water, finding it too much of an effort.

She had never imagined however that in a yacht one could have a bath fixed to the floor in a special cabin of its own.

That was what she was looking at now and she saw it was rather a strange shape being very deep and not very long.

There was also a basin that was fixed to the

148

wall, which she had expected.

A jug of water standing in it had a top to prevent the water from spilling out.

She washed her face and hands and felt better.

Then very carefully, because the ship was heeling over, she slipped back into bed.

It was a large and comfortable bed, and the sheets and pillow-cases were of the best linen.

The blankets she was aware were new, and had never been washed.

She thought as she looked around her that everything seemed new and she suspected therefore that the *Ulysses*, was a new acquisition.

Bowers came back with a tray in his hands. He was moving she thought very skilfully, considering he had to walk at an angle.

He put the tray down on the bed and she saw that everything on it had covers so that nothing could spill over.

Bowers looked at her and said:

'Yer Ladyship looks a bit chilly. I think I saw somethin' when I unpacked that'll keep you warm.'

He opened a drawer that was fitted into the wall like everything else in the cabin.

After rummaging around he brought her

what she saw was a velvet stole to wear over an evening-gown.

As it was a pale blue and trimmed with maribou, she thought it very glamorous and it was certainly warm as she put it round her shoulders.

'Thank...you.'

'Now eat up!' Bowers said firmly, 'and when I comes back, I'll tell Your Ladyship what you wants to know.'

He grinned at her and went away.

Valessa though he was rather like a kindly Nanny, and she did not feel in the least embarrassed by him.

Because she felt hungry she explored what he had brought her to eat. There was plenty of it, and very delicious.

As they were breakfast dishes, she thought, although she did not ask the time, that it must be morning, and she had therefore slept all night.

Twenty minutes later Bowers returned.

'Feelin' better, M'Lady?' he asked.

'Yes, very much better, thank you,' Valessa answered. 'I am sorry to be such a nuisance.'

'It's no trouble,' Bowers said, 'and wot you've got to do, M'Lady, if you'll forgive me sayin' so, is to fatten yourself up a bit.'

He gave a little chuckle as he went on:

'When I takes off your gown and puts you to bed last night, you looked so thin, I thought you'd disappear!'

Valessa laughed.

'I am sure I shall soon get fat if I eat such delicious food as you have just brought me!'

'It'll be luncheontime in a bit over an hour.'

'Do you...think,' Valessa asked hesitatingly, 'that...His Lordship will...expect me to...dress and...join him?'

She did not know quite how to express it and there was a perceptible pause before she said the last two words.

'I thinks, M'Lady, you'd best stay where you be,' Bowers replied, 'at least until you feels better than you are now.'

He picked up the tray, steadying himself rather like an acrobat as he made for the door.

Then he said:

'I'd keep out o' the way o' His Lordship, and give 'im time to get used to it, so to speak!'

He was gone before Valessa could think of anything to say, but she could understand his reasoning.

She was sure the Marquis was hating her violently, and she had no wish to encounter him until things were better.

She remembered how angry he had seemed when they were driving towards London.

She felt her whole being shrinking from the fury which, when they met, she feared would break over her head.

'Bowers is right,' she told herself, 'I am not well enough to get up.'

She snuggled down against the pillows.

When Bowers came back with her luncheon she was sound asleep.

Afterwards it seemed to Valessa extraordinary that she had managed for three days to stay in her cabin seeing nobody but Bowers.

She slept most of the time.

He woke her up and made her eat her meals, which she did obediently.

Mostly because she did not wish to disappoint him.

Then actually being far weaker than she had realised, she went back to sleep.

She enjoyed the movement of the ship.

It made her think of the swing her father had made for her.

It had hung on the branch of a large tree in the garden when she was a little girl.

He would swing her up and down until it felt as if her toes could touch the sky.

She would move so fast that she thought she was flying.

The *Ulysses*, built to the Marquis's own

specifications, was very large and very sturdily built.

Later Valessa was to discover that it had many gadgets and innovations aboard which no other English yacht had.

It had survived the elements in the Bay of Biscay without anything getting broken.

They were fortunate in that they had the right wind to carry them through it at an almost unprecedented speed.

When finally the sea was calmer and the sun much warmer, Bowers came in to say:

'How's aboot gettin' up today? It's as warm as Spring, an' I'm waitin' for Your Ladyship to see the rest of th' cabins.'

'I...I think I am...too lazy to get up,' Valessa replied.

What she meant was that she was too frightened.

Every day that passed without seeing the Marquis made her dread the fact that she ever had to do so.

The idea of him seemed to grow in her until he over-shadowed her like a huge monster, or the Ogre in the Fairy Tales she had read as a child.

She had thought then that the Ogre was a giant.

While the little boy or girl which she identified with herself were tiny creatures about the size of his finger.

'Now come along, M'Lady,' Bowers was saying, 'you musn't lose the use of your legs.'

'If I do, I will have to be pushed around the deck in a wheel-chair!' Valessa said without thinking.

Then she remembered the Marquis being pushed by Lord Cyril in a wheel-chair.

'Wot I was goin' to suggest,' Bowers was saying, 'is that I run Your Ladyship a bath. It'll be a cold one, but th' sea water's ever so good for the skin.'

He did not wait for her reply.

He had obviously given orders that some cans of water were to be brought to the Cabin for Valessa heard him taking one from a steward.

Then Bowers poured it into the strange-looking bath.

She thought it must be like the Chinese ones which her father had described to her as being very deep but short.

The person taking a bath sat on a seat so that the water came nearly up to his neck.

When she went into her little bathroom she found the the water was not high enough for that but it was exciting to lower herself down into the deep bath.

She did not mind the water being cold, having always had cold baths at home.

When she got out she felt invigorated and more alive than she had felt for a long time.

Bowers had laid out her clothes on the bed and chosen for her a pretty gown she had never seen before.

It was made of a woollen material and had a wrap rather like the one she had been wearing. It was made of the same stuff and had a long fringe.

She thought the gown must have been very expensive.

She felt not so much resentful at wearing Lady Sarah's clothes as embarrassed.

She wondered what she should do if the Marquis told her to throw them overboard.

Then she knew that once again she was letting her imagination run away with her and he would certainly not suggest anything so stupid.

When finally she was dressed, her eyes were dark and wide with fear. They seemed to fill the whole of her face.

She looked at herself in the mirror and decided that she no longer had the ashen pallor she had seen before.

Her skin had in fact, a translucent whiteness about it, and there was also a touch of colour in her cheeks.

She took a deep breath.

'Now,' she told herself, 'I have to face the Ogre!'

She went from her cabin, putting out her hands to steady herself on each side of the passageway.

Then she climbed the companionway.

At the top of it she saw Bowers waiting to open the door of the Saloon.

That was where the Ogre would be waiting to gobble her up!

CHAPTER SIX

The Marquis was overwhelming.

He was standing at the end of the Saloon as Valessa entered and she thought he was even larger and more menacing than she had expected.

She stood looking at him, holding onto the frame of the door for support.

It seemed to her as if he grew larger and larger until he *was* the Ogre.

'Come and sit down!' he said sharply.

She could no longer look at him as she moved across the Saloon to sit down on a chair opposite him.

He crossed his legs and sat back in the chair and she thought he looked like a Judge who was about to pass sentence on her for being a criminal.

As she waited she was aware that her heart was beating tempestuously and her hands were trembling.

'Well, let us get it over!' he said. 'How much do you want?'

Valessa looked at him in surprise.

157

'I...I do not...understand!' she stammered as he was obviously waiting for a reply.

'Of course you do!' he said contemptuously. 'This is blackmail, and I presume there is nothing I can do but pay you.'

The way he spoke was unbearably insulting.

Valessa felt a pride she did not know she possessed rise within her breast.

In a voice that was a little stronger and not so faltering she answered:

'If you think...I am asking...you for...money you are...mistaken!'

'You *are* asking me for money,' he insisted, 'unless you think I shall accept you as my wife, which I have no intention of doing!'

Valessa dropped her eyes and was silent.

After a moment he said:

'How could you have done anything so appalling, so revolting, as to trick me into a Marriage Service?'

'I...I did not know...I had no idea,' Valessa faltered, 'that it was anything more than a... charade which Sir Harold...told me was... arranged to...amuse Lady Barton's...guests.'

'You expect me to believe that?' the Marquis asked.

Now he was sneering and Valessa thought no man could be more unpleasant.

'I expected to hear a lot of lies from you,'

he went on, 'but you can hardly imagine I will believe them! So let me repeat—how much do you want?'

'As I...told you...I want...nothing,' Valessa said. 'I was...going to ask you...but you... would not...listen...if you would...take me...to my...home.'

'Where is that?' the Marquis asked. 'In the slums of Lambeth or the filth of St Giles's?'

Now the way he spoke left Valessa speechless.

She had heard her father talk of the appalling conditions in both places and how they were a breeding-ground for pick-pockets, thieves and murderers.

'If you will...listen to me,' she said after a long silence, 'I...I will try to...explain.'

'I do not want your explanations!' the Marquis snapped. 'What I want to hear is what you craftily planned with Lady Barton to humiliate me!'

'No...no...that is not...true!' Valessa cried.

As if the Marquis could not control himself, he suddenly rose to his feet.

'Stop lying, damn you!' he shouted. 'Let us "get down to brass tacks". You want money? Very well, I will pay anything to be rid of you!'

The way he roared at her and the expression of hatred in his eyes made Valessa give a cry.

It was like the sound of a small animal caught in a trap.

As if she could bear it no longer she rose and ran across the Saloon.

Then as she went through the door she saw to the right of her was another door leading out onto the deck.

She was completely distraught and the Marquis had frightened her to the point where she could no longer think clearly.

She felt despairingly there was only one way to escape him.

She pulled open the outer door.

Because they were moving fast and the sea was comparatively calm the yacht was fairly steady.

The railings were just ahead of her and Valessa ran to them.

She held onto the top rail, then realised that her skirt was too tight for her to throw herself over it into the sea.

She therefore started to climb up the first, then the second bar.

She heard a voice shouting from behind her and thought it was the Marquis.

She bent forward to throw herself head first into the waves.

As she did so the sails swung over and the yacht heeled over onto the other tack.

It threw Valessa backwards and as it did so somebody caught hold of her and pulled her down on the deck.

'What are you doing, you little fool!' the Marquis asked furiously.

It was then, because his grip hurt her, that she lost control of herself and was aware only of her fear as she broke down.

'Let me...die!' she sobbed. 'I want to...die!'

The Marquis did not reply, he merely picked her up in his arms and carried her back into the Saloon.

She was crying so helplessly that she was hardly aware of what he was doing. He set her down on the chair she had just vacated.

She only knew that the whole world seemed dark and terrifying and she cried convulsively with her hands over her face.

The Marquis stood looking at her for a moment, then he went to the cupboard in the corner of the Saloon.

He opened it.

There was a row of bottles, all held in place so that they could not be upset by the roughness of the sea.

He poured a little brandy into a small glass, then shutting the door of the cupboard took it back to her.

'Drink this!' he commanded.

Valessa did not answer, she merely shook her head, her hands still over her face.

As the yacht was now rolling a little the Marquis sat down beside her.

'How could you think of doing anything so foolish,' he asked, 'as to try to drown yourself?'

'I...want to...die!'

As an afterthought, and as he did not speak, she added:

'You will...then be...free of...me.'

The Marquis looked at her in surprise. Then he said:

'You are thinking of me?'

'H.how...could I have...guessed they would ...plan anything so...wicked?' Valessa sobbed.

Her tears seemed to come ever faster as she stammered:

'I was just going to...kill myself anyhow... when they came...to the house...but they... stopped me.'

'Why were you going to kill yourself?' the Marquis asked.

He was speaking quietly and calmly, but Valessa could not control her tears.

After a moment he said:

'Stop crying, then perhaps you can tell me exactly what happened.'

'You...had better...let me...die!' Valessa whispered.

'If you had drowned yourself as you were trying to do,' the Marquis said, 'I should certainly
have been charged with your murder!'

Valessa was suddenly still.

What she had heard him say seemed to stop
her tears as if she had had a sudden shock.

She took her hands from her eyes.

'Did...did you say you would be...charged
with murder?' she asked hesitatingly.

'I am quite certain Lady Barton and, of
course, Grantham, would convince their friends,
if not a Jury, that I had conveniently disposed
of you!'

Valessa stared at him.

'I...I am sorry,' she faltered.

Looking at her almost for the first time, the
Marquis thought he had never seen anyone
look so pathetic.

There were tears on her cheeks, her eye-
lashes were wet.

When she stood at the railings, the spray
from the waves had splashed over her hair and
the front of her gown.

He saw that her lips were trembling.

Because she was looking at him questioningly
he said:

'I am sure you are intelligent enough to
realise that the two people I have just mentioned are my implacable enemies.'

'But...I have no...wish to...hurt you,' Valessa faltered. 'I just thought...if I died...then you...would be...glad.'

'As I have already told you, I would be labelled a murderer for the rest of my life, even if I was not charged with the crime.'

'I...I never...thought of...that.'

She spoke in a helpless way and she was suddenly aware of her tear-stained cheeks and fumbled for her handkerchief.

The Marquis took a white linen one from his pocket and handed it to her.

It smelt of *Eau de Cologne* and made her think of her father, and she wanted to cry again.

She wiped her eyes, then blew her small nose as a child might have done.

The Marquis held out the glass of brandy.

'Take just a few sips,' he said, 'and you will feel better.'

Because she was still too afraid to argue with him, she did as he told her.

Then he took the glass in which there was still quite a lot of brandy and put it down on a table which was battened to the floor.

He sat down again and after a moment said:

'Suppose we forget what I said to you just now, and start from the beginning?'

'I am...frightened!'

'Of me?'

'Y.yes...I knew...you would be...very...very angry...and...gobble me...up!'

She spoke without thinking and there was just a touch of amusement in his voice as the Marquis said:

'So you think I am an Ogre!'

Valessa nodded, and again wiped her eyes.

She felt better after the brandy and was still ashamed of the way she had broken down.

She was quite certain her father would have disapproved, and she knew men hated a scene.

She clasped her hands together and in a small voice that was like a child's she asked:

'If I tell...you exactly...what occurred...will you believe...me?'

'I will try to,' the Marquis said, 'and I shall know if you are not telling the truth.'

'I always...tell the...truth,' Valessa said with unexpected dignity. 'Papa and Mama...hated ...liars.'

'Your parents are alive?'

'N.no...they are...both dead.'

It would have been impossible for anyone not to recognise the agony and despair in her voice.

'I am sorry, but surely you do not live alone?' the Marquis asked.

'I have...no money,' Valessa replied, 'and when Papa was...killed his...creditors came and...took away all...the furniture there was ...in the...house!'

The Marquis stared at her as if he found it hard to believe what she was saying.

'Because I was so hungry, I knew the...only thing I could...do was to...drown myself in the...river.'

There was silence, then as she glanced at the Marquis she saw he was looking at her gown.

She knew he was thinking that she could not be telling the truth when she was dressed as she was now.

He would also have noted the smart coat she had worn when he was driving them to London.

'What I am...wearing...now,' she explained, 'belonged to...Lady Barton. She gave me...the clothes to...wear at...The Towers, as well as...some money.'

She thought as she spoke that the Marquis would denounce her once again as being a charlatan.

Instead he said quietly:

'You have not yet told me how you met Lady Barton.'

'She...she came to my house just...when I was...about to...walk to the...river,' Valessa said, 'that is if I...could manage...to get... there.'

'Why did she come to your house?'

'She had...a fall out...hunting and hurt her arm. The Gentlemen with her...asked for... bandages.'

'Now I understand,' the Marquis said. 'And you had not met her before?'

'No, but because my home is only...about five miles from...the Towers, I had...of course ...heard of her.'

As she spoke, Valessa hoped that the Marquis would believe that she had not come from Lambeth or St Giles.

He was thinking over what she had just told him, and he said:

'You bandaged Lady Barton's arm. Then what happened?'

'I know...now,' Valessa said in a frightened tone, 'that I should have...guessed what would ...happen when I overheard her saying...you had told her...she was not..."good enough" for...you.'

The Marquis's lips tightened.

Then he asked, still in that quiet voice:

'What else did she say?'

'After Lord Cyril had imitated you...'

Valessa gave a sudden cry.

'Of course! It was very...stupid of me not to ...realise it...before, but it was...he who made ...your responses in...the Chapel! He spoke...

exactly like...you.'

'I guessed that was what must have happened,' the Marquis said dryly. 'I remember how skilfully he imitated everybody when we were at School together.'

'It was very...very stupid of me...I see that ...now,' Valessa said, 'but I was feeling...so ill ...and my brain did not seem to be...working.'

'I suppose that is understandable,' the Marquis said.

She thought he spoke reluctantly.

'I thought...they would...leave,' she went on hastily, 'but instead Sir Harold...came into the kitchen and said that...Lady Barton would... give me £200 if I would...take part in a... charade to...amuse her...guests.'

She looked at the Marquis pleadingly.

'I swear to...you,' she said, 'on everything I...hold Sacred, that I did not...know what they were...going to do...until the very last ...moment.'

She thought the Marquis was looking grim and with a little sob she said.

'I...I can see now...why what they...planned could not...take place the...first night at...the Towers, because they were...waiting for...the Special Licence!'

She spoke the last words a little incoherently and in such a low voice that she thought the

Marquis had not heard her.

She could remember all too clearly that ghastly moment when she had come back to consciousness and found herself on the bed beside the Marquis.

She shivered in horror at the memory of Lady Barton and her friends jeering at them.

She could see Sarah Barton laughing and holding up the Marriage Certificate and the ugly, spiteful expression on her face that seemed to contort it.

It was impossible to say any more.

She knew that what she had done was unforgettable and once more she put her hands up to her face.

'If I cannot...die,' she asked, 'what can I.... d.do to make...things better for you?'

The Marquis did not answer, and after a moment Valessa went on:

'Perhaps...if I stayed somewhere...abroad...I could find...work...then in a year or so...you could say I had...died.'

There was silence after she had spoken and at last the Marquis asked:

'What sort of work are you suggesting you could do?'

Valessa sighed.

'I have...thought of...this before. When they had finished with...me at...the Towers...I meant to...go to London with the...money Lady Barton had...given me to...visit one of... the Domestic Agencies.'

She was thinking it out, as she had before.

'As I look too young to be...a Governess I thought perhaps...I could be a...companion to an old lady and read...to her...or whatever it is companions do.'

She was unaware that the Marquis was watching her.

There was a curious expression in his eyes, as if he still thought she might be play-acting.

At the same time, he was almost convinced she was not.

'I am sure...someone would...want me,' Valessa went on bravely, 'and the...two hundred pounds would last...a long time in Italy or...perhaps in Greece.'

'And if it did not,' the Marquis said, 'what would you do then?'

Valessa made a helpless little gesture with her hands before she said:

'That would not...worry you...and I am sure I...could manage for a...year. Then you...could say I had died...of...some fever.'

'It might be from the starvation you said you were suffering from when Lady Barton arrived at your house.'

He saw an expression of fear in Valessa's

face. Then she said:

'I will...manage...I am sure I can manage...somehow.'

'By yourself?'

'It will be difficult, because I have...always been...with Papa...but I am nearly...nineteen ...and I should be able to...look after myself.'

The Marquis rose to his feet.

As the yacht was moving smoothly he walked to the port-hole to look out to sea.

Valessa knew he was thinking.

But as he stood there she could not help remembering how magnificent he had looked on *Saladin* and how exciting it had been to watch him win the Steeple-Chase.

'I want...him to...believe me!' she told herself.

He walked back to her and again sat down in a chair.

'I have been thinking over what you have told me,' the Marquis said, 'and I believe you!'

He saw Valessa's eyes light up.

'You do? You...really...do?' she asked. 'I promise you...that I have...told you...the truth!'

'I think I would know if you were lying,' the Marquis said, 'and I therefore suggest that we forget Lady Barton and never mention her again.'

Valessa drew a deep breath.

Then, as she would have spoken, the door of the Saloon opened and a steward came in.

He walked to the Marquis's side to say:

'Chef says, M'Lord, that luncheon will be ready in five minutes, an' I wondered if I might lay the table?'

'Yes, of course,' the Marquis agreed.

He turned to Valessa to say:

'I had no idea it was so late. I expect you would like to tidy yourself, and I hope you will eat with me?'

For the first time Valessa thought of her appearance, and put her hands up to her hair.

It had been made wet by the spray, and she was sure her eyes needed bathing.

She hurried below to find Bowers tidying her cabin.

'You all right, M'Lady?' he asked.

'Yes...I am all right...thank you,' Valessa replied.

She went into the small bathroom to wash her face.

Then because she did not wish to keep the Marquis waiting, she hurriedly tidied her hair and went back to the Saloon.

The stewards had already laid the table which was arranged to one side of it.

The Marquis was drinking a glass of champagne, but when he offered Valessa one she shook her head.

'I think I should have something to eat first.'

The Marquis raised his eye-brows and she explained.

'I had food at the Towers, but it was the... first time after having had very...little for so ...long.'

She gave him a quick glance before she added:

'I drank on the way to London to keep myself awake, but I am sure it is...something I should...not do...otherwise.'

'I understand your reasoning,' the Marquis said, 'and I think you are very sensible.'

He put down the glass he was holding in his hand and said:

'As it happens, I seldom drink during the day because I want to keep myself fit for riding. But I felt after the dramatics of this morning I needed a little sustenance!'

He smiled at Valessa as he spoke and it took the sting out of the words.

She gave him a shy little smile in return, then sat down at the table opposite him.

After the steward had brought in the food which was, she realised, quite exceptionally good, the Marquis talked.

173

Inevitably, Valessa thought, it was about horses and especially *Saladin*.

He told her where he had bought him when he was only a yearling, and how exciting it had been to watch him develop.

'I was praying he would win the Steeple-Chase,' Valessa said simply.

'It was something I really wanted to do,' the Marquis admitted.

'I kept wishing that Papa was there and he could see you. He would have been as excited as I was.'

'Your father was keen on horses?'

'He was a very good rider, and he made what income we had after Mama died by buying horses cheaply and training them until he could sell them for quite a lot of money.'

The Marquis thought that was what quite a number of men had tried to do, mostly unsuccessfully.

He was watching Valessa all the time he was talking.

He was finding it more and more difficult to understand how she could have become embroiled in the dastardly plot thought up by Sarah and Harry.

He found it hard to believe completely in her story of being penniless.

It was even harder to credit that in consequence she had been on the verge of suicide.

One thing however was obvious: she did not come, as Sarah had said she did, from the gutter and it was difficult to believe she was not a Lady.

He listened to the way she spoke and realised she was educated and there was not the trace of an accent in her voice.

He also noticed the way she ate.

She did nothing that would not have been approved of in the most distinguished social circles.

His brain told him there must be a snag somewhere.

But his instinct was sure he could accept her story and that she was telling the truth.

As they talked Valessa seemed to have lost most of her shyness.

He realised too there was no longer the terror in her eyes there had been when she looked at him.

The Marquis could be very beguiling when he tried and by the end of luncheon Valessa was talking to him as she would have talked to her father.

She had had little or no social experience since her mother had died.

She therefore found it fascinating to be alone with a very handsome man even though she admitted she was afraid of him.

Yet it was delightful to have him talk to her as if she was his equal.

The Marquis found she was knowledgeable in a way he would not have expected.

When he talked of his visiting Italy she spoke of the history of Naples.

She spoke of how the Greeks and Romans had left behind the ruins of their Temples and Villas.

The Marquis told her how he had visited Pompeii and she said with a little shiver:

'I have often thought of the horror the people must have experienced as they found themselves choking to death in an atmosphere suddenly thick with volcanic ash.'

When luncheon was over the Marquis thought she looked tired, and he sent her to her cabin to rest.

'Tomorrow we shall be in smoother water,' he said, 'and then I am sure you would like to come out on deck.'

'I would like that,' Valessa said, 'and Bowers has told me of the many gadgets you have installed in your yacht. I would love to see those too.'

When she went below, the Marquis sat for a long time alone in the Saloon thinking about her.

His thoughts were very different from those which had darkened his mind and infuriated him all the time he was driving to London and for the first days of the voyage.

Instead of a common harlot, who was intending to extort huge sums of money from him or, worse still, flaunt herself as the Marchioness of Wyndonbury, he was confronted with a young girl.

As he watched and listened to Valessa he found it impossible to believe that she was not what she appeared to be.

Which was somebody young, very innocent, and deceived rather than deceiving.

It was such a complete *volte face* that he found himself bewildered and not at all certain what he should do about it.

He had thought when he came abroad to escape the mockery of his friends that he would somehow be able to bribe himself out of the situation.

He had told himself he would give this woman who had been foisted upon him as his wife, an enormous allowance on condition that she stayed out of England.

He would still be married to her. But at least he would not have to see her or be continually humiliated by her behaviour.

The only alternative, he knew, was to

challenge the legality of the marriage.

He had been aware before Valessa realised it that it was Cyril Fane who had impersonated him in the Chapel.

It was he who had made the responses which the Clergyman believed came from the Marquis.

He knew however, all too well, the publicity such a case would create.

The way he would be laughed at and undoubtedly lampooned for having been drugged and manipulated by people he thought were his friends.

The idea made him shrink in horror.

Either way, whatever he did, the whole thing would be a disgrace not only to himself, but to his family.

As he thought it over, he was astutely thinking that perhaps by some miracle he might manage to avoid the worst of the situation.

Valessa was very young. Surely he could teach her how to behave decently?

If she was at all intelligent she could act the part of a Lady and get away with it.

The more he thought of the situation, the more this seemed to be the only possible answer.

It was something that had not occurred to him until now after he had met Valessa.

There was certainly nothing notably vulgar about her.

When she had cried, she had seemed little more than a child who had got into trouble through no fault of her own.

He found himself feeling sorry for her.

How was it possible she had been on the verge of suicide because she had no money and no food?

How was it possible that she was prepared to die rather than face his anger?

How was it possible she had wanted to set him free?

The Marquis was used to dealing with people of all sorts and conditions.

He had been noted as an exceptionally good officer because of the way he looked after the men under him and understood them.

He was now almost convinced that Valessa was not deceiving him.

He was also aware that when she had washed and bathed her eyes and come back into the Saloon for luncheon, she had looked very lovely.

At the same time she was rather as if she had been battered about by forces over which she had no control.

He had been genuine in his efforts to set her at ease.

He thought he had been successful when before he sent her below to lie down she had said with a shy little smile:

'Thank you...thank you very much for... being so kind...to me.'

'What I must do,' the Marquis finally decided, 'is to gain her confidence and her trust, then mould her into being at least presentable in public.'

At the same time he felt the fury of his anger seething once again inside him.

He knew that while he was out of England, his relatives would undoubtedly hear of what had happened.

As far as Valessa was concerned, they would inevitably be outraged.

'They will hate her for what they think she is,' the Marquis told himself, and knew that whatever he did, the future was very problematical.

Now he made up his mind.

He was determined to mould Valessa into at least a very good imitation of what he expected of the Marchioness of Wyndonbury.

He decided the first thing would be not to continue to talk of what had occurred.

He would try, if it was possible, to forget Sarah Barton and what was a diabolical revenge.

But he knew he would find it even harder to forget Harold Grantham.

He admitted to himself that Harry had some justification to dislike him, for having taken away Yvonne.

At the same time, his behaviour was not that of a Gentleman.

The Marquis knew that he himself would never have stooped so low as to humiliate another man with whom he had been at School.

They also belonged to the same Clubs.

The Marquis was wise enough to know that hating anyone would not undo what had been done.

It would only make it impossible for him to be at his ease with Valessa.

He was aware, when she dined with him, that she had an instinct or a perception which had surprised him.

He knew it was as difficult for him to deceive her as it was for her to deceive him.

She was looking extremely attractive in a pink gown which must have cost an enormous amount of money and was really too smart to be worn in a yacht.

But the Marquis, experienced where women were concerned, realised that Valessa had put it on because it gave her confidence.

Bowers had told her before she left her cabin:

'You looks like flowers, M'Lady, an' that's the gospel truth!'

'Thank you,' Valessa smiled, 'I only hope... that is what...His Lordship will...think too.'

''E's in a different mood this evening,' Bowers confided. 'I don't know wot you said t'him, but he's almost like his old self.'

Valessa thought her heart leapt. If the Marquis had forgiven her she need not be so afraid.

He was certainly charming when she entered the Saloon.

They sat down to dinner and he began talking again of things that interested him.

She told him a little shyly how she had loved the stories of the gods of Olympus and found he was as knowledgeable as her mother had been about them.

They talked about Egypt, where the Marquis had been.

He found she had read the history of the Pyramids and the stories of the Temples in Luxor.

The Marquis noticed how her eyes would light up when they discussed things which he had found in the past were of little interest to other women with whom he had dined.

They were intent only on attracting him and receiving the compliments they thought of as their right.

He was aware now that everything they said was to Valessa quite impersonal.

He was sure by the end of dinner that she had never given a thought to herself or her appearance.

Two days later they sailed into the Mediterranean Sea.

The Marquis found himself thinking that if he had to have a female aboard his yacht, it would be hard to find a more congenial companion than Valessa.

She made no demands upon him.

She did not expect him to compliment her, but she did want to listen to him.

She was very interested when he showed her parts of the yacht at which other women he knew would not have given a second glance.

He was astonished how much she had read about the countries at the far end of the Mediterranean.

He realised that her father was widely travelled and she was of course repeating what he had taught her.

At the same time he could see that she thought for herself.

The questions she asked him were so intelligent that he thought they might almost have come from one of his men-friends.

Sometimes they argued.

The Marquis was aware that Valessa talked to him in the same way as she had talked to her father when he was alive.

As they sailed on the Marquis told himself with a mocking smile that for the first time in his life he was with a young and attractive woman who did not desire him as a man.

He was aware that Valessa looked at him with admiration.

When she spoke of the way he rode there was a note almost of admiration in her voice, and she thought there was something God-like about him.

It was a position, he thought with amusement, that he had to share with *Saladin*.

He and his stallion were indivisibly linked in Valessa's mind.

Lying in bed he found it hard to sleep.

The Marquis had never in his life been in a position where a woman was concerned only with his brain rather than his heart.

He knew that Valessa watched him, after she had said something provocative or unusual, to see his reaction.

She waited eagerly for his reply because it appealed to her mind.

He knew he was not mistaken in thinking that they had become what he might call "friendly". Yet her heart had not for one

184

second beaten quicker because he was near her.

Nor had her lips suggested that he should kiss them.

He thought he knew every movement a woman could make when she was attracted by him.

The way her hands would go out to touch him.

The glance she would give him from under her eye-lashes.

The very conscious movements of her body which were an invitation in themselves.

Valessa might, he thought, have been talking to a Professor eighty years old or as she had told him so often in their discussions with her father.

The Marquis began to think that he had met the one woman in the whole world who was immune to his charms.

It was a somewhat sobering thought.

He almost wanted to reassure himself by being in the company of the Beauties he was sure were pining for him in London.

Then he knew that tomorrow Valessa would come eagerly into the Saloon for breakfast.

Her eyes would be shining with excitement.

She might have seen a porpoise or had her first sight of the Pyrenees.

Whatever it was she would bring the sunshine with her.

'She is certainly very unusual!' the Marquis said to himself.

Then unaccountably, he wished the night would pass quickly so that he could be with her again.

CHAPTER SEVEN

'Tomorrow,' the Marquis said to Valessa, 'we go ashore at Marseilles.'

He did not say any more.

The steward was offering them a dish of the delicious food they enjoyed every night.

Valessa felt as if she had stopped breathing.

She had been so happy for the last week as they had sailed round the end of Spain and into the Mediterranean.

The weather had been unprecedentedly warm for November and the sunshine made everything glitter with a golden aura.

The sea was calm and very blue, the colour of the Madonna's robe.

To Valessa it was all entrancing.

She found too it was an excitement she had never anticipated to talk to the Marquis, to listen to him.

He could tell her so much she wanted to know and she thought it was like having an Encyclopaedia all to herself.

He was so understanding that she almost forgot why she was on the yacht with him.

He said they would not speak or think of Lady Barton again and he had kept his word.

He never referred to what had happened at Ridgeley Towers, or to any of the people who had been there.

Valessa was desperately afraid that any mention of it would bring back his anger.

She therefore really tried to put it from her mind.

Only at night did she ask herself how long she could continue to be so happy.

It was obvious that the Marquis could not go sailing about the world for ever.

He had great responsibilities in England and she was sure he missed his horses.

At the back of her mind there had always been a dark, threatening idea that he might, as she had suggested, leave her in some foreign country.

She thought now that he would give her a little money for when the £200 that was sitting in her dressing-table drawer ran out.

Perhaps he would send it to her on a monthly basis.

But it was not money she wanted; it was the security of being with him.

It was terrifying to think of being alone in a country where she knew nobody.

Everything had been very different when she

travelled with her father and mother.

That was so many years ago and she had been so young that she could hardly remember it.

Since then she had just lived in the peace and quiet of her home and after her father's death she had seen no one.

That was why she knew everything that had happened had been a surprise.

In fact, so surprising that she had not realised what was actually happening, when the 'pretend marriage' turned into a real one.

'I am the Marquis's wife,' she told herself, 'but he will never acknowledge me!'

When she thought of leaving him there was a strange pain in her heart.

On board he would rise early in the morning and she would hurry to get ready to have breakfast with him.

Then they would go out on deck and he would explain to her where they were.

He had shown her the new gadgets with which he had equipped the *Ulysses* and she thought they were amazingly clever.

Her father had been a clever man, but she knew he was not as erudite as the Marquis.

It had been her mother who had taught her about Literature. It was fascinating to find how much it interested him.

She had been lulled into believing that her

feelings of security and happiness would go on forever.

Now it would end tomorrow.

'Where shall I go?'

'What shall I do?'

The questions repeated themselves over and over in her mind.

She thought frantically that she must savour every moment of the last hours that she was with him.

She knew that when he left her it would be all she would have to remember.

She stood on deck looking at the coast of France.

She wanted to order the yacht to sail slower so that it would take months or even years before they reached Marseilles.

They had taken longer on the voyage than was really necessary.

When they were into the Mediterranean the Marquis had ordered the Captain to drop anchor every night.

This meant they moved nearer to land, found a small bay or a fishing-port, and stayed there until morning.

They usually anchored too late at night for Valessa to go ashore.

The Marquis also thought it too cold for her, and he would leave the yacht and walk for an hour or more so as to exercise himself.

Valessa found it impossible to sleep until she heard him return.

She would listen to his footsteps in the passage and hear him coming to his cabin.

Then he would talk to Bowers while he undressed.

Only when the valet had left him and there was silence did she fall asleep feeling secure because she was near him.

But in the future she would be alone.

She felt her whole being cry out at the idea and the fear was back in her eyes but the Marquis did not notice.

They went below to change for dinner, Valessa hurried so that she would not miss even a second of being with him.

Usually he was quicker than she was.

Tonight she had put on the first gown she took down from her wardrobe.

Only when she glanced at herself in the mirror did she realise it was a very pretty one of blue silk, the colour of the sea.

Its puffed sleeves, Valessa thought, looked like the waves.

It was very simple to have been Sarah's taste. Yet it looked exactly right on Valessa.

It made her skin seem dazzlingly white and reflected the colour of her eyes.

Because she had been feeling happy, and because the food aboard the yacht was superb, she had put on a little weight.

The lines had gone from her face and her cheeks were rounder. She no longer looked weary or on the edge of exhaustion.

She was not aware that Bowers had said to the Marquis:

'If you asks me, M'Lord, 'Er Ladyship's on the point of 'avin' a nervous breakdown, an' if we're not careful we'll 'ave her sufferin' from Brain Fever!'

This had made the Marquis even more determined not to upset her.

He remembered how desperate she had seemed when she had tried to throw herself into the sea.

He found sometimes that the fear he had seen in her eyes when she had first come into the Saloon was haunting.

He blamed himself for what had happened afterwards.

Valessa was very different from the blackmailing houri he had expected her to be.

When dinner was over and a steward had removed the table they anchored unexpectedly early. There was a bay with cliffs rising above a sandy beach.

Valessa heard the anchor go down and as she

turned her head the Marquis said:

'Would you like to go out on deck? It is much warmer tonight and we shall be sheltered by the cliffs.'

'I would love it!' Valessa exclaimed.

She picked up the stole that went with her gown.

Bowers had made her carry it with her but she had not needed it at dinner.

It was of blue velvet in the same colour as her gown, and it was bordered with, to her astonishment, ermine.

It seemed incredible that Sarah Burton should have given away anything so expensive.

But Valessa knew it was of no consequence to her since she was so rich.

She put the robe round her shoulders and looked expectantly at the Marquis.

They went up on deck.

Valessa saw that in the star-studded sky there was a full moon which was reflected in the calm sea.

It was so beautiful that she could only stare in wonder, thinking it was a Fairyland she had only seen in her dreams.

Then as she stood looking up at the moon she remembered her conversation the first night at Ridgeley Towers.

It had been the man sitting next to her,

although she had never learnt his name.

'My advice to you, Miss Chester,' he had said, 'is not to fall in love with Stafford Wyndonbury.'

Valessa remembered thinking it was a strange thing for him to say.

'I was not thinking of falling in love,' she had answered, 'but of course, you are right. It would be a tragedy for anyone to love "The Man in the Moon"!'

It was a phrase she had used to herself to describe people who were out of reach.

As the memory of it came back to her, she thought what an apt description it was.

The Marquis, though he was kind and understanding, was always, she thought, a being apart from the ordinary world.

He was out of reach and not really human.

She threw back her head to look up at the moon and had no idea that the Marquis seeing the long line of her neck and the perfection of her features thought how very beautiful she was.

In the daytime her hair, which had almost a magnetic buoyancy about it, seemed to have captured the sunlight.

Now it was silver and even more becoming.

Without really thinking of it he moved a little nearer to her, leaning against the railing.

She had placed both her hands lightly on it, as she looked upwards.

'What are you thinking about?' he asked.

'The Man in the Moon!' she replied.

'Why should you hanker after him when there is another man beside you?' the Marquis asked.

As he spoke he put his arms around her and before Valessa could realise what was happening, his lips took hers captive.

For one moment she was still with astonishment.

Then her Fairy-Story had come true.

The 'Man in the Moon' was kissing her and it was even more wonderful than it had been in her dreams!

The Marquis was at first very gentle because he was afraid of frightening her.

He felt the softness and innocence of her lips and without her being aware of it her whole body seemed to melt into his.

His kiss became more demanding, more possessive.

It was what he had wanted for a long time, but would not admit it.

Now because Valessa had looked so beautiful, so desirable, he was unable to control himself.

As he kissed her he knew that what he was

feeling was different from what he had ever felt before with any other woman.

He wanted to make love to her and the blood was throbbing in his temples.

At the same time he wanted to protect her, and he was thinking of her rather than himself.

It had been impossible to be alone with her all this time without realising that she was very intelligent.

She however knew nothing about a man's desire for a woman, or a woman's for a man.

What was real to her was the ideal love eulogised by poets and expressed by musicians.

It was something that had excited her mind but never touched her heart.

The Marquis held her closer still.

He knew what he wanted more than anything else in the world was for Valessa to respond to him. To think of him and love him as a man.

To Valessa, it was as if Apollo himself had come down from the skies.

Or, as she had been thinking, the 'Man in the Moon', who was a god.

To her the Marquis was not a man, but a supernatural being so wonderful that she wanted to worship him.

Then as he went on kissing her she felt sensations she had never imagined.

They rose through her body and were an

ecstasy beyond words.

It was like the shafts of light pouring from the moon and was rapture to which her whole body vibrated.

Then the moonlight seemed to burn its way from her breasts to her throat and from her throat to her lips.

It was so unutterably marvellous that she thought she must have died and was in a Heaven that she never knew existed.

Only when the Marquis raised his head did she realise incredibly that this was love.

She had never thought that love could be like this.

But she loved him, and there was no world, no sky, nothing except him.

The Marquis saw her eyes looking up at him with an unmistakable expression of admiration. Very gently he released her.

As he did so, he was desperately afraid she would be frightened of him.

He knew that her first kiss had been a wonderful emotional experience.

Yet because he was able to read her thoughts, she was still in Fairyland and not yet aware that she was human.

They stood looking at each other for what seemed a long time, but was really only a few seconds.

Then the Marquis in a voice that seemed strange even to himself said:

'Goodnight—Valessa.'

He walked away.

She watched him go, but he did not look back.

Then with a murmur that was a sound of sheer joy she left the deck.

She lay in bed feeling the Marquis's arms were still around her, his lips still on hers.

Never had she believed that anything could be so wonderful.

'I love...him! I...love him!' she said beneath her breath and she thought her father and mother were listening.

This was real love, the love she had longed for and thought she would never know.

She was in love with 'The Man in the Moon' and he had kissed her.

The rapture of it made her feel she was flying up into the sky to touch the moon, and the stars enveloped her.

'I love him!' she told herself and thought no one could be more blessed than she had been.

She heard the Marquis come to bed and prayed that he was thinking about her.

She knew it would be impossible for him to feel as she did.

Yet he had given her something so priceless that she felt it was a gift from God.

It never entered her mind that she might go to him and ask him to kiss her again.

Nor did she think that because they were married, there would be nothing wrong in her doing so.

The Marquis was still the 'Man in the Moon', and out of reach.

Yet he had kissed her.

To Valessa his kiss was like the moonlight, it was not of this earth, but from the sky above.

In his cabin the Marquis was fighting against going into Valessa's cabin and kissing her again.

He wanted her so violently that only his iron self-control prevented him from doing so.

He admitted to himself that he was in love.

He had also had a long experience with women.

Valessa was so innocent and so idealistic that he knew he would have to treat her in a different way from any other woman he had ever met.

He wanted her to love him.

He wanted not only her body, but her heart and her soul.

Yet he was aware because she was unawakened that this would not happen overnight.

With a faint smile he told himself he had to woo her and it was something he had never had to do before.

Always he had been the one who had been wooed, pursued, and finally seduced.

Now his role was very different.

To Valessa he was a god, and he knew perceptively that she would never make any advances to him.

It was, he thought with a faint touch of amusement, a reversal of everything he had ever known.

When he had walked away from Valessa and left her alone on the deck it had been an agony for him to do so.

But he was aware that it would make her think of him.

Perhaps she would want him to go on kissing her and would begin to think of him as a man.

He tossed and turned in his bed, finding it impossible to sleep.

He told himself that of all the experiences of his life, this was the strangest.

He, the most sought-after man in London, who was talked about behind his back as a 'Don Juan', a 'Casanova', was now in a very different situation.

He was using his instinct as well as his brain to make a young girl love him.

He thought his friends would find it amusing.

He had been with her for nearly two weeks and not by a flicker of her eye-lashes had she shown that she wanted him to touch her.

The Marquis was aware she had not the slightest idea what happened when a man and a woman made love.

After all the sophisticated, overwhelmingly passionate women he had known, it would be a new experience he had never even thought about.

To teach a completely innocent girl about love.

'I want her love,' he said to himself in the darkness, 'I want it, and God knows, I will try to win it.'

He thought of how many things he had won.

Not only women, but horses, Steeple-Chases, and a hundred other prizes with his expertise.

Now, at this moment, he was uncertain of himself, afraid that if he frightened Valessa she would run away from him.

She might even drown herself as she had tried to do before.

If that happened how could he bear it?

'Oh, God, help me!' the Marquis murmured.

It was the first prayer he had said for a very long time.

When Valessa woke she felt as if the sun was shining not only outside but also within her body.

She would not have been surprised if, when she looked in the mirror, she had seen it radiating from her in golden rays which Greeks believed came from the solar plexus.

When she went into the Saloon for breakfast her eyes seemed to fill her face.

She looked at the Marquis who was already sitting at the table and she wanted to go down on her knees.

She wanted to thank him and burn frankincense in front of him as the Ancient Greeks had done to their Gods.

Instead of which she gave him a shy smile as he rose perfunctorily before she sat down.

A steward hurried to bring her an English breakfast and some fragrant coffee.

She was aware as she looked out to sea that the yacht was sailing into the port of Marseilles.

Suddenly she felt as if a cold hand clutched at her breast.

It flashed through her mind that the Marquis had kissed her last night to say goodbye.

'How...can I...bear it...if that is...what he... intends?' she asked herself.

Then she knew that if that happened she

202

must be brave and not make a scene.

It was what she had suggested herself, and it would in fact, set him free.

No one would think anything unpleasant about him if her death was announced in a year's time.

She could not eat any more because she was afraid.

Then the Marquis said:

'I think we shall be ashore in about twenty minutes.'

Valessa drew in her breath.

She waited for him to tell her more, but instead he went on:

'It is a lovely day, and I think when the sun grows stronger it will be quite hot.'

He rose to walk to the port-hole.

'The Captain says,' he continued conversationally, 'that he has never known such good weather at this time of the year.'

'Perhaps...we are...lucky,' Valessa murmured.

'I am sure we are,' the Marquis replied.

The *Ulysses* glided gracefully into port and in a few minutes she would be tied up beside the Quay.

'It is an excuse for wearing your prettiest bonnet,' the Marquis said lightly.

Without answering him Valessa went below

where she expected to find Bowers packing her trunks.

Her cabin was, however, exactly as she had left it, and with a leap of her heart she hoped she was not after all expected to leave at this moment.

Perhaps the Marquis was taking her to see some house where she could stay.

At least until she found herself the job she had talked about and she would have one more day with him.

'Please...God...do not...let me have to... leave him,' she prayed. 'Please...God...let him ...keep me in the yacht for a...little while... longer.'

She felt as if her whole being went up to Heaven in a passionate plea.

Even as she prayed she thought that once again the Marquis was out of reach.

She was praying for the moon and she had been warned not to fall in love with the man in it.

'I shall...never forget...him,' she thought despairingly.

She had put on this morning one of the prettiest gowns amongst those she had been given.

It was white with a very full skirt and a blue sash.

The bonnet which matched it was decorated with cornflowers.

There were even little satin slippers of the same colour.

When Valessa went upstairs the Marquis thought he had never seen her look more lovely.

Then he had to look away, otherwise he knew he would have to kiss her.

To Valessa his gesture, and the fact that he did not compliment her, merely confirmed that he was out of reach.

They got into the open carriage that was waiting for them on the Quay.

As they did so she thought no man could look more handsome.

Once again she was praying she could stay with him today.

The carriage drove off and she looked back at the port and the shimmering blue of the sea.

'That is Devil's Island over there,' the Marqui was saying again conversationally, 'where the criminals are imprisoned, and from where they can never escape.'

Valessa shivered.

It was something she did not want to talk about.

They drove on.

The horses turned in through the impressive

gates with the Union Jack flying outside the distinguished-looking house. Valessa realised it was the British Consulate.

As the carriage came to a standstill outside the front door the Marquis said:

'There is no need for you to get out. I am collecting my letters, which I told my Secretary to send here, and also I hope, the British newspapers.'

A number of uniformed servants bowed him into the Consulate and Valessa sat waiting.

She thought there was an eagerness in his voice when he spoke of the British newspapers.

She was sure he wanted to go home.

'Perhaps he will...leave me...tomorrow,' she thought despairingly.

Then she was praying that he would stay a little longer.

The Marquis was no longer inside.

He had no wish to see the Consul, and a secretary had handed him several packages.

One contained his letters and several larger ones he knew contained newspapers.

He was wondering if there would be anything in them about himself.

He only hoped that neither Sarah nor Harold Grantham would have been so indiscreet as to have talked to journalists.

He hoped that Sarah would not wish her part

in the deception to be made public knowledge.

A flunkey took his parcels from him and followed him as he went towards the door.

Outside another carriage had come up behind his and a lady alighted from it.

The Marquis was looking at Valessa and he started when a voice exclaimed:

'Stafford! I was not expecting to see you here!'

He turned to see the *Duchesse* de Savalon, and as he lifted her hand to his lips she went on:

'How could you come to this part of France without telling me! But perhaps you have only just arrived.'

'I came into port only an hour ago,' the Marquis explained.

'Are you telling me you are not staying?' the *Duchesse* said. 'Because if you are, I must give a special dinner-party for you.'

The Marquis realised this was a special privilege.

In France the *Duchesse* de Savalon was of great importance. Although she was nearing sixty, there were still traces of the great beauty she had been when she was young.

She was one of those remarkable Frenchwomen who swayed the Political management of the country.

She had a Salon in Paris to which anyone who

207

was of any importance fought for an invitation.

She had always been a great friend of the Marquis's father, whom he had always suspected to have a very tender spot for her in his heart.

She had often stayed at Wyndonbury and the Marquis knew she was a close friend of Queen Adelaide.

'Now, when will you come to me?' the *Duchesse* was asking.

As she spoke her eyes were not on him but on Valessa.

Valessa had been waiting impatiently in the carriage for the Marquis to return.

She was now sitting as near as she could to the door and looking at him eagerly.

Her face was framed by her pretty bonnet and she was looking exquisitely lovely in the morning sunshine.

The Marquis was just wondering how he could refuse the *Duchesse* without appearing rude when she exclaimed:

'Surely—but I cannot be mistaken! This is Charles Chester's daughter!'

Valessa heard her and impulsively got out of the carriage.

A footman had already opened the door for the Marquis.

'Did you know Papa, *Madame?*' she asked eagerly.

'Then you *are* Charles Chester's daughter!' the *Duchesse* exclaimed. 'You are exactly like your mother! In fact you still look as you did when you stayed with me in Paris all those years ago!'

'I remember! Of course I remember now!' Valessa replied. 'You had a huge dolls'-house in the Nursery!'

The *Duchesse* laughed.

'It is still there and my grandchildren adore it, just as you did!'

The Marquis was speechless and looking astonished. The *Duchesse*, seeing his expression laughed.

'You are thinking it is clever of me to recognise Valessa after all these years, but she is exactly like her mother who was one of the most beautiful people I have ever seen!'

Before the Marquis could say anything the *Duchesse* went on:

'But tell me, child, why are you here. And is your father with you?'

'Papa is...dead,' Valessa said, a little sob in her voice.

'Oh, I am sorry!' the *Duchesse* exclaimed, 'then...?'

She looked at the Marquis for explanation,

and at last he found his voice.

'Valessa is my wife.'

'Your wife?' the *Duchesse* repeated. 'But that is wonderful! I often wondered, Valessa, what had happened to you, and that you should marry Stafford seems to me quite perfect!'

She put her hand on the Marquis's arm.

'You will both dine with me tomorrow night,' she said, 'and I will not let you refuse. My son will be thrilled to see you, and so will Marguerite, who always loved Elizabeth.'

She gave a little laugh before she added:

'And of course, we all loved Charles, who was sometimes a very naughty boy, but how could we ever be angry with him?'

She turned to Valessa.

'Goodbye, me dear, I shall see you tomorrow night at seven-thirty, and do not be late! In the meantime, I will find a wedding-present for you!'

She moved away, then stopped.

'Oh, by the way, I have just remembered— the death of Valessa's grandfather was in the newspapers last week. As you have been at sea, perhaps you have not heard about it. He was a very old man, so it was not unexpected.

She walked on without waiting for a reply.

Valessa got back into the carriage and the Marquis sat beside her. He was stunned for a moment by what he had heard.

Then in a voice that sounded strange even to himself he asked:

'How is it...possible that your parents...knew the *Duchesse* de Savalon?'

'To be truthful,' Valessa replied, 'I did not recognise her until she spoke to me, but I had never forgotten the dolls'-house.'

'But—you were in Paris?' the Marquis persisted.

'It was years ago, and I was only about seven at the time,' Valessa replied, 'but Papa used sometimes to speak of her.'

The Marquis was bewildered.

As they drove on he was thinking of how particular the *Duchesse* had always been about who she knew.

He had known women weep because they had not been invited to one of her parties.

When she came to England she stayed at Buckingham Palace and not in the French Embassy as might have been expected.

He remembered what Sarah had said about Valessa.

He did not however ask any further questions until they were back in the yacht.

They went up the gangway and into the Saloon. There the steward put the newspapers and letters down on the table and the Marquis said:

'What was the *Duchesse* saying about your grandfather being dead? Who was he?'

'I...I have never...met him,' Valessa replied.

'Never met him!' the Marquis exclaimed.

'Papa ran away from home because he did not wish to be a soldier, and Mama went with him because they were already in love.'

The Marquis was opening the newspapers.

As he had expected, his Secretary had sent him both *The Times* and the *Morning Post* for every day since he had left England.

They would have taken at least a week to reach Marseilles.

He thought therefore the last newspaper that had been dispatched might be the one of which the *Duchesse* spoke.

He opened *The Times* on the *Obituaries* page, but Valessa said in a small voice:

'Papa...changed his name when he...ran away...there is no use therefore in you looking under "Chester".'

'Then what was your Grandfather's name?' the Marquis enquired.

'He was...General Sir Montgomery Chesterton-Huntley!'

The Marquis stared at her in sheer astonishment.

'H.he was very...angry with Papa for not...

obeying him,' Valessa said nervously.

'He commanded the Life Guards!' the Marquis said. 'And his eldest son, who I suppose is your Uncle, is now in command. I served under him!'

'He never spoke to Papa,' Valessa said defiantly.

'But you are still part of the family,' the Marquis remarked thoughtfully, almost to himself.

He threw the newspapers down on the table and said:

'I think, Valessa, you should have told me about your family.'

Valessa was taking off her bonnet.

'You did not...ask me,' she said a little nervously, 'and...I was afraid you might be... angry.'

'Why should I be angry?'

'Because you...told me not to talk about Lady Barton...but I...wanted you to know I was not...what she...said I was.'

'I thought it would upset you to even think about it,' the Marquis said self-effacingly, 'but now tell me exactly who you are.'

He saw that Valessa was nervous.

At the same time, he sensed that she wanted him to know that she was a Lady, and not the disreputable creature whom Sarah had described.

213

'Papa...as you now know,' she said in a small voice, 'was the...second son of my grandfather ...he was cut off without a shilling...which was why we were so poor...and I have always... h.hated them for being...so unkind.'

'I can understand that,' the Marquis said, 'and who was your mother?'

'Her father was Lord Ardleigh,' Valessa replied, 'but he too never spoke to...Mama, after she...ran away.'

She looked up and saw that the Marquis was staring at her in sheer astonishment.

'Lord Ardleigh?' he repeated. 'Are you sure?'

'Yes...of course I am sure! Mama was the Honourable Elizabeth Leigh...but she never used her title. They were just "Mr and Mrs Chester"!'

'Lord Ardleigh—your grandfather—is a first cousin of my mother's!' the Marquis exclaimed.

He thought as he spoke that this was the miracle for which he had prayed.

A miracle which would make his family accept Valessa gladly as his wife.

He could hardly believe what he was hearing.

He had never for a moment thought that Valessa was as well born as he was himself.

'I think both my grandfathers were—very

214

cruel,' Valessa was saying. 'If I ever had children, I would never throw...them out of my life...however badly they behaved.'

'Your father and mother ran away together because they loved each other,' the Marquis said in a low voice.

'They loved each other so much that nothing else mattered,' Valessa answered, 'not even that Mama was engaged to be married to somebody very important, and the marriage was due to take place two weeks later.'

'They were happy?' the Marquis asked.

'Mama said that being with...Papa was like... being in...Heaven!'

There was a little lilt in Valessa's voice which the Marquis did not miss.

'Is that what you want to feel?' he said quietly.

Valessa looked away from him.

The Marquis realised she was shy and thought her so utterly adorable that it was with difficulty that he did not sweep her into his arms.

The stewards were preparing the table so he said:

'You must tell me all about it later.'

At luncheon Valessa told him how her father had wanted to travel all over the world.

How at first, after she was born, they had

215

taken her everywhere with them.

The Marquis could understand why she had wanted to learn so much about the countries where she had been.

She had been at the time, too young to remember much about them.

'I think I must have been about six or seven years old when they took me to Paris,' Valessa was saying, 'and we stayed with the *Duchesse*.'

She paused as if she was thinking and then went on:

'Then I remember when we went to Rome. I thought the Colosseum was very big, and I was frightened in case the lions and tigers were still there, waiting to tear me to pieces!'

The Marquis laughed.

She went on to tell him of how after her mother died her father spent all the capital from which her allowance had come.

'He was utterly and completely...miserable without Mama,' she said. 'It was impossible for him to think clearly...but only to suffer.'

She thought that was what she would feel if she lost the Marquis.

He was listening to her.

But his eyes kept going to the clock on the mantelpiece and she thought he must have an appointment to keep and wanted to be rid of her.

'If you are going ashore,' she said, 'perhaps I should go to...lie down.'

It was something she had done on Bowers' instructions every day they had been at sea.

She hoped the Marquis would say she could go with him.

Instead he replied:

'That is a good idea.'

He rose to his feet.

'Go and lie down,' he said, 'then I will come and tell you my plans.'

'I would...like...that,' Valessa said eagerly.

She hurried to her cabin where the port-holes faced out to sea and the sun was shining through them.

She took off her pretty gown and hung it up in the cupboard. Then as she usually did, she put on her night-gown and got into bed.

Most afternoons she had slept a little.

This made her feel brighter and more quick-witted when she had driven with the Marquis.

She heard him go into his cabin, then a few minutes later there was a knock on her door and he came in.

To her astonishment she saw he was wearing a long robe like the one her father used to wear.

It touched the floor, and fastened with braided buttons high up to the neck.

He shut the door and came towards her.

217

She thought there was a strange expression in his eyes she had not seen before.

'I thought...you were...going ashore,' she said.

'I have changed my mind,' the Marquis replied. 'I thought for a change we might tonight have dinner at a Restaurant. I believe there are some very good ones in Marseilles.'

'In a...Restaurant?' Valessa exclaimed.

It was something she had never done and knew it would be very exciting.

What was more, she would be with the Marquis and he was not sending her away—not yet.

He sat down on the side of the bed facing her, then he said:

'As we may be late, I thought that as you were resting I might do the same. Perhaps we could rest together.'

She felt her heart give an excited leap.

Then she realised his lips were very near to hers and she felt the same thrilling sensations running through her as there had been last night.

'I...I would...like that,' she whispered.

'Are you sure?' the Marquis enquired.

She looked into his eyes and could not look away.

'I do not want to frighten you,' he said.

'I am not...frightened with...you...how could ...I be?'

She thought he would kiss her and her lips trembled. Instead he took off his robe and got into bed beside her.

For a moment she could hardly believe it was happening.

Then as very gently he put his arms around her she made a little murmur and hid her face against his neck.

'I wanted to hold you like this last night,' the Marquis said, 'but I was afraid if I came to your cabin you would think of me as an Ogre!'

'Not as...an Ogre,' Valessa whispered, 'but ...as "The Man in...the Moon"!'

'Why the "Man in the Moon"?'

'Because he is...out of...reach.'

He pulled her a little closer.

'I am not out of reach, Valessa, and I want to kiss you!'

He waited.

Very slowly, because she was shy, she turned her face up to his.

He felt her tremble and knew it was not with fear.

Then slowly, as if he wanted to savour the moment, his lips were on hers.

Valessa knew this was what she had wanted.

She had been so desperately afraid when he kissed her last night that his kiss had meant goodbye.

Instinctively, without thought, she moved nearer to him.

His heart was beating against hers.

She felt that both the moon and the sun were shimmering through her body and she was no longer herself, but his.

She did not understand her feelings. But she wanted to give him not only her lips, but her heart and everything else that was hers.

She wanted to become a part of him, to be even closer than they were at the moment.

He kissed her eyes and as he did so she said:

'I...I love you...I...love you!'

'That is what I want you to say,' the Marquis answered, and his voice was very deep and unsteady.

'I...I did not...know that...love was...like this,' Valessa whispered.

'Like what?'

'I feel as if I am no...longer me...but belong ...to you, and as you...are in the...moon, then I must be...there...too!'

'My precious love,' the Marquis said, 'how could I ever be alone again without you?'

Then he was kissing her straight little nose, her cheeks and the softness of her neck.

It was then that Valessa felt as if the sun had turned to fire.

Her whole body was burning with a strange ecstasy.

It made her want something which was out of reach.

Yet in some strange way it was the Marquis.

'I want you,' he said, 'God, how I want you! But you must help me, my lovely one, to be very gentle and not frighten you!'

'I am not...afraid.'

'Are you quite, quite sure.'

'Quite sure...but please...go on loving me... and kissing me.'

She lifted her lips once again saying:

'I...I thought you were...going to...leave me.'

'I will never leave you,' the Marquis said. 'You are mine, my lovely one! Mine for all time...and for ever!'

'I...I can stay...with you?'

'You can stay with me so that I can teach you about love.'

'That is...what I...want! Teach me...teach me and make me...love you as you...want to be...loved.'

'I just want you as you are,' the Marquis said.

He thought as he spoke that she was perfect and everything he had ever wanted in his wife.

But how could he have imagined for one instant that he would find her in such strange circumstances?

He knew, although it did not really matter, that he had 'turned the tables' completely on Sarah and Grantham.

When they learned to whom they had married him, they would know they had made fools of themselves.

Sarah's revenge was as far as he was concerned, very sweet.

It was of no consequence, he thought, who Valessa was or where she came from.

His love was so great that if she had really come from the gutter he would still have loved her.

But from her point of view, although she would not understand that she was who she was, it made all the difference.

No one would hurt her, no one would sneer.

His family would be delighted that his wife was related to them by blood and that her grandfather was so distinguished.

The Marquis knew he had won again.

Yet nothing mattered except that Valessa should be happy.

He would protect her, look after her and love her for the rest of their lives.

He knew because they had both suffered,

that they would be better parents to their children.

Also kinder to people who searched for love, as they had done.

Then because Valessa was so soft and sweet and had ignited a flame within him he was kissing her again.

He kissed her until they were together in the moon, which shone far above the mundane world, and were in fact as gods.

Valessa's heart was beating as frantically as his and her breath was coming quickly from between her parted lips.

Her eyes were shining with a radiance which came from God.

The Marquis very gently, very lovingly made her his.

Now the sun was casting its golden glow all around them.

The fire from it burnt through their bodies, their hearts and their souls. It lifted them in a spiritual ecstasy up into the sky.

They were in the moon where nothing could hurt them and their love encircled them like stars.

It was a love that would grow and strengthen all through their lives.

A love which would carry them into eternity together.

MAGNA-THORNDIKE hopes you have enjoyed this Large Print book. All our Large Print titles are designed for easy reading, and all our books are made to last. Other Magna Print or Thorndike Press books are available at your library, through selected bookstores, or directly from the publishers. For more information about current and upcoming titles, please call or mail your name and address to:

MAGNA PRINT BOOKS
Long Preston, Near Skipton,
North Yorkshire,
England BD23 4ND
(07294) 225

or in the USA

THORNDIKE PRESS
P.O. Box 159
Thorndike, Maine 04986
(800) 223-6121
(207) 948-2962
(in Maine and Canada call collect)

There is no obligation, of course.

F,